John Baldwin Buckstone

Married Life

A Comedy in Three Acts

John Baldwin Buckstone

Married Life
A Comedy in Three Acts

ISBN/EAN: 9783744788205

Printed in Europe, USA, Canada, Australia, Japan

Cover: Foto ©Andreas Hilbeck / pixelio.de

More available books at **www.hansebooks.com**

MARRIED LIFE

A COMEDY IN THREE ACTS

BY

JOHN BALDWIN BUCKSTONE

New American Edition, Correctly Reprinted from the Original Authorized Acting Edition, with the Original Casts of the Characters, Synopsis of Incidents, Time of Representation, Description of the Costumes, Scene and Property Plots, Diagrams of the Stage Settings, Sides of Entrance and Exit, Relative Positions of the Performers, Explanation of the Stage Directions, etc., and all of the Stage Business.

NEW YORK
HAROLD ROORBACH
PUBLISHER

MARRIED LIFE.

CAST OF CHARACTERS.

	Haymarket Theatre, London, Aug. 20, 1834.	Park Theatre, New York, Feb. 2, 1835.
MR. SAMUEL CODDLE	Mr. Farren.	Mr. Matthews.
MR. LIONEL LYNX	Mr. Webster.	Mr. Mason.
MR. FREDERICK YOUNGHUSBAND	Mr. Vining.	Mr. Ritchings.
MR. GEORGE DISMAL	Mr. Brindal.	Mr. Latham.
MR. HENRY DOVE	Mr. Buckstone.	Mr. Fisher.
MRS. SAMUEL CODDLE	Mrs. Glover.	Mrs. Wheatley.
MRS. LIONEL LYNX	Mrs. Faucit.	Mrs. S. Chapman
MRS. FREDERICK YOUNGHUSBAND	Mrs. Humby.	Mrs. Harrison.
MRS. GEORGE DISMAL	Mrs. Tayleure.	Mrs. Vernon.
MRS. HENRY DOVE	Mrs. W. Clifford.	Mrs. Gurner.

TIME OF REPRESENTATION—TWO HOURS.

SYNOPSIS OF INCIDENTS.

MR. and MRS. LYNX, having discussed a conjugal breakfast, are visited by MR. and MRS. CODDLE, an oddly assorted couple, just before MR. LYNX departs for the day. As the latter is pre-eminently a ladies' man, his wife jealous by nature, and MRS. CODDLE personally attractive, the two ladies fall afoul of each other with slight provocation. An encounter of alarming proportions is terminated by the appearance of MR. and MRS. YOUNGHUSBAND, a newly married pair perpetually interrupting and contradicting each other, who drop in with some information of interest which is confirmed by MR. and MRS. DOVE—the latter an ex-school-marm constantly drilling her lord in politeness and correct pronunciation which the poor man, who had been her former footman, cannot comprehend. It transpires that MR. LYNX had formerly placed at MRS. DOVE's school a young lady whose present whereabouts is unknown. This mystery so enrages Mrs. LYNX that she invites all her friends to dine with her the next day, in order to overwhelm her volatile spouse with a public exposure of his villainy. LYNX now returns to his house and finds his wife possessed of embarrassing information, but promises to be on hand to justify himself at dinner the next day. At this juncture Mr. Coddle comes back, is drawn aside by Lynx, made aware of the latter's secret and the impossibility of its explanation, and consents, on pain of having a little secret of his own proclaimed, to assume his friend's burden by declaring, when the time comes, that the mysterious young lady is his own daughter.

Mr. Coddle's situation overpowers him with such nervous agitation as to excite his wife's suspicion and her resolve to wring a confession from him. His apprehension is visibly heightened at learning from Mr. and Mrs. Dismal of an elderly lady in black, of masculine appearance, who has just arrived from foreign parts in quest of a delinquent husband. After exacting their silence in this tale of horror and despair, Mr. Coddle summons all his fortitude and precedes the others to the house of Mr. Lynx, with assumed gaiety but direful forebodings. The guests are all assembled, the dinner takes place and Mr. Lynx vindicates his conduct to the satisfaction of everybody except his wife; but Mr. Coddle's Nemesis overtakes him in the shape of a letter to Mrs. Coddle from the elderly lady in black, in which the latter claims to have been married to the monster twenty years back. Then follows a general explosion. Mrs. Coddle bids her treacherous Samuel an eternal farewell; Mrs. Lynx having laid bare her lord's supposed perfidy, quits his house forever, while he in disgust, starts in another direction never to return; Mr. and Mrs. Younghusband, catching the infection, separate after a spirited wrangle; the Dismals flounce out in opposite ways after concluding that they were a couple of old fools to marry at all; and Mr. Dove, having been wounded in a tender point, departs in a passion, leaving his better half in a state of utter collapse.

Mr. Coddle having taken to flight and changed his name, now secretes himself in an obscure location with the intent of living in future by candle light. While bewailing his unhappy plight he is unearthed by Mr. Lynx, who is followed by Messrs Dismal and Younghusband. As the unhappy wretches are reflecting what indispensable comforts wives are, Mr. Dove arrives with intelligence that the· elderly lady in black is not the first Mrs. Coddle at all, whereupon he is dragged out by the now ecstatic Coddle to discover and satisfy the lawful Mrs. Coddle; the other men being advised to seek and become reconciled to their wives as well. Meanwhile the five ladies hold an indignation meeting which is dissolved in tears. Mr. Lynx now seeks his wife and clears up the mystery of the young lady at school. Mr. and Mrs. Younghusband adjust their differences happily; the Dismals are reunited in cheerfulness; Mr Dove forgives his Martha, who promises never to correct him again; and Mr. Coddle in all the conscious pride of innocence, becomes reconciled to his wife, and sets an example of the way that all matrimonial quarrels should end, which the others follow. Their conjugal joy is now complete, and their lesson has taught that the best of happiness is found in a loyal and affectionate Married Life.

COSTUMES.

N. B. *For the convenience of managers two sets of costume sare indicated. Those pertaining to the time of its original production may, per-*

haps, be more consonant with the spirit of the play, though many companies will prefer modern dresses. The following costume plots have been prepared expressly for this edition of " MARRIED LIFE *" by* THE EAVES COSTUME COMPANY, *No. 63 East 12th Street, New York, from whom all costumes may be hired at reasonable charges.*

ORIGINAL—1834.

MR. CODDLE.—*1st Dress:* Long drab greatcoat, with gray spencer (a short overcoat) worn over it; drab pantaloons; colored gaiters; broad-brimmed hat; Welsh wig (a worsted cap); large comforter or woolen scarf around neck. *2d Dress:* Blue swallow-tail coat with brass buttons; satin waistcoat; gaiter-pantaloons; stock and collar. *3d Dress:* Nankeen frock coat and gaiter-pantaloons; white waistcoat; ruffled shirt-front; straw hat.

MR. LYNX.—*1st Dress:* Morning gown, afterwards changed for walking coat; light waistcoat and pantaloons; gaiters; stock and collar. *2d Dress:* Brown swallow-tail coat with brass buttons; satin waistcoat; gaiter-pantaloons. *3d Dress:* Same as first.

MR. YOUNGHUSBAND.—*1st Dress:* Blue frock coat; satin waistcoat; tight buff pantaloons; Hessian riding boots. *2d Dress:* similar to LYNX's second dress. *3d Dress:* Similar to first.

MR. DISMAL.—Same dress throughout. Black frock coat with rather long skirts, black waistcoat and pantaloons; white gaiters; low-crowned black silk hat. Hair worn long and dark.

MR. DOVE.—Same dress throughout. Plum-colored frock coat with short skirts and tight sleeves; tight-fitting pantaloons; Buff waistcoat, white beaver hat.

MRS. CODDLE.—White muslin or other summer-like costume; white satin bonnet.

MRS. YOUNGHUSBAND.—Silk dress and bonnet of the period.

MRS. DISMAL.—Silk dress and bonnet of quaint style.

MRS. DOVE.—Silk dress and bonnet of yellow or some other showy color.

MRS. LYNX.—Silk dress and bonnet of the period.

MODERN—1889.

MR. CODDLE.—*1st Dress:* Long ulster and pea-jacket or large plaid shawl worn over it; dark trousers; arctics (overshoes); knotted worsted cap; long woolen muffler; soft wide-brimmed hat, woolen mits and gloves. *2d Dress:* Dark frock coat; figured waistcoat; dark brown trousers and gaiters, stock and collar. *3d Dress.* Linen suit; straw hat; light necktie; low shoes. This costume to present the greatest possible contrast to his first dress.

MR. LYNX.—*1st Dress:* Modern smoking jacket (afterward changed for coat); fancy modern waistcoat, trousers and neck scarf. *2d Dress:* Black evening suit. *3d Dress:* Ordinary walking suit.

MR. YOUNGHUSBAND.—*1st Dress:* Morning suit, light overcoat and derby hat. *2d Dress:* Black evening suit. *3d Dress:* Modern walking suit.

MR. DISMAL.—Black frock coat, with long skirts, waistcoat and trousers; black stock; drab gaiters; characteristic black silk hat. Hair rather long.

MR. DOVE.— *1st Dress:* Plaid suit, rather loud in style; bright necktie; white gaiters; characteristic hat. *2d Dress:* Very exaggerated evening costume. *3d Dress:* Similar to first.

MRS. CODDLE.— *1st Dress:* Very thin and summery walking dress and hat. *2d Dress:* Dinner costume. *3d Dress:* Same as first.

MRS. LYNX.— *1st Dress:* Handsome morning gown. *2d Dress:* Dinner costume.— *3d Dress:* Stylish walking suit.

MRS. YOUNGHUSBAND.— *1st Dress:* Stylish walking suit. *2d Dress:* Handsome dinner gown. *3d Dress:* Same as first.

MRS. DISMAL.—Old-fashioned silk dress, bonnet, etc.

MRS. DOVE.— *1st Dress:* Very showy walking costume. *2d Dress:* Elaborate dinner gown, pronounced in style and color. *3d Dress:* Same as first.

PROPERTIES.

ACT I.

Breakfast and service on table, L. C. Bell rope by fireplace. Bell outside. Watch and newspaper for LYNX. Furniture as per scene-plot.

ACT II.

SCENE 1.—Book for CODDLE. Letter, glass of water and shawl for MRS. CODDLE. Furniture as per scene-plot. Curtains at windows.

SCENE 2.—Chair. Letter for MRS. LYNX.

SCENE 3.—Envelope containing a letter and marriage certificate. Letter for MRS. LYNX. Dessert, etc., on table. Furniture as per scene-plot.

ACT III.

SCENE 1.—Two candles burning on table, C. A hammer, a skewer and some tow. Furniture as per scene-plot.

SCENE 3.—A chair.

STAGE SETTINGS.

ACT I.

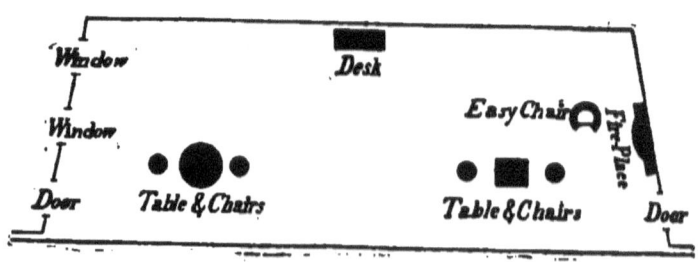

ACT II.—*Scene 1.*

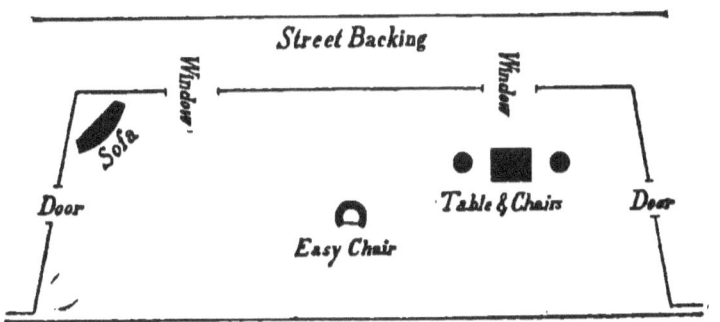

ACT II.—*Scene 3.*

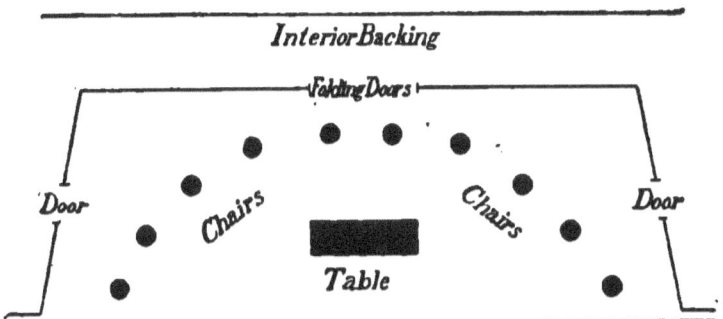

ACT III.—*Scene 1.*

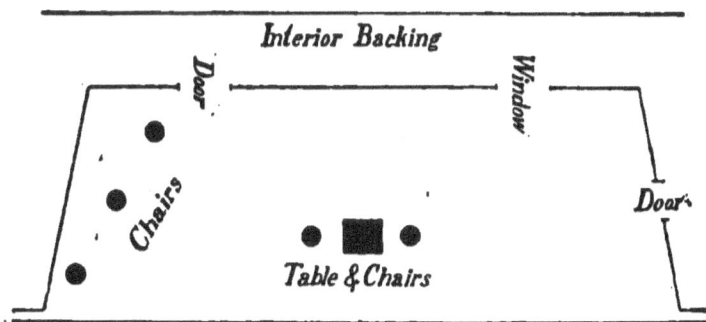

SCENE PLOT.

Act I.

An apartment at the house of MR. LYNX. Fancy chamber in 3 G. Doors R. 1 E. and L. 1 E. Fireplace L. 2 E. Practicable windows R. 2 E. and R. 3 E. Desk C., against flat. Easy-chair before fireplace. Table and 2 chairs L. C. Small table and chair R. C.

Act II.

SCENE 1.—An apartment at the house of MR. CODDLE. Fancy chamber in 3 G. Street backing in 4 G. Windows, with curtains, R. and L. in flat. Doors, edged with list and leather, R. 2 E. and L. 2 E. Easy chair C. Table and chairs L. Sofa up R.

SCENE 2.—A room at LYNX'S. Plain chamber in 1 G. Entrances R. and L.

SCENE 3.—Drawing-room in 3 G. Interior Backing in 4 G. Folding doors C., in flat. Doors R. 2 E. and L. 2 E. A large table C., on which is set out a complete dessert, and table appointments. Semi-circle of 10 chairs.

Act III.

SCENE 1.—A meanly furnished room in 3 G. In the flat are a door, R., and a window, with closed shutters, L. Door with practicable bolt, L. 2 E. Table and chairs C. 3 chairs R.

SCENE 2.—A room at a boarding house, in 1 G. Entrances R. and L.

SCENE 3.—A gallery in the boarding-house. Interior in 3 G. Practicable doors in the flat, R. and L.

STAGE DIRECTIONS.

The player is supposed to be facing the audience. R. means right ; L. left; C., center; R. C., right of center; L. C., left of center; D. F., door in the flat or scene running across the back of the stage; R. F., right side of the flat; L. F., left side of the flat; R. D., right door; L. D., left door; C. D., center door; 1 E., first entrance; 2 E., second entrance; U. E., upper entrance; 1, 2 or 3 G., first second or third grooves; UP STAGE, towards the back; DOWN STAGE, towards the footlights.

R.   R. C.   C.   L. C.   L.

MARRIED LIFE.

ACT I.

Scene.—*An apartment at the house of* MR. LYNX. LYNX *is discovered in his morning-gown reading a newspaper before the fire.* MRS. LYNX *at a small table,* R., *in the sulks.*

Lynx. (*reading*) "BOW STREET.—*Matrimonial Squabble.*—The chief magistrate was occupied all the morning investigating a case of assault, arising out of a matrimonial squabble. It appears that the wife of the complainant is a woman of violent passions, and so excessively jealous, that her husband's life is endangered." Do you hear that, my dear? You are not singular in your temper, you see.

Mrs. Ly. Indeed!

Lynx. There are other women in the world excessively jealous besides yourself.

Mrs. Ly. You think so, do you?

Lynx. Shall I read the whole of the police report?

Mrs. Ly. You may do just as you please.

Lynx. Don't you feel interested in the case? Have you no sympathy with the poor woman?

Mrs. Ly. You have taken good care to destroy all my sympathy; indeed, almost every feeling and quality that I once possessed.

Lynx, Save one, my dear.

Mrs. Ly. Well, sir, what is that one?

Lynx. The quality of making yourself extremely disagreeable —why don't you take breakfast?

Mrs. Ly. I don't want any.

Lynx. You did not sup last night.

Mrs. Ly. I did not require it.

Lynx. You ate nothing at dinner yesterday.

Mrs. Ly. I had no appetite.

Lynx. You'll starve yourself, love, and die.

Mrs. Ly. Then you will be happy.

Lynx. I shall certainly lead a quieter life——

Mrs. Ly. And have more opportunities for carrying on your intrigues.

Lynx. What intrigues, dear?

Mrs. Ly. Those are best known to yourself.

Lynx. I thought you were perfectly acquainted with them.

Mrs. Ly. I am acquainted with a sufficiency, believe me.

Lynx. Name them, my dear.

Mrs. Ly. I shall not trouble myself so much.

Lynx. Nay, I insist.

Mrs. Ly. Well, then, sir,—my dressmaker could not call yesterday, but you must make yourself ridiculous.

Lynx. What did I do?

Mrs. Ly. You told her, in my presence, that she was very pretty.

Lynx. Was there any sin in that?

Mrs. Ly. 'Twas not only a very great familiarity on your part, sir, but a want of respect for me.

Lynx. True—it was wrong in me to forget that few women can endure to hear another admired.

Mrs. Ly. And few men think their wives to be possessed of any charms superior to the first doll they may meet.

Lynx. Excellent, indeed—my love, we must turn authors, and between us publish a book of Conjugal Aphorisms. However, I plead guilty to your first charge, and implore your mercy—proceed to the next.

Mrs. Ly. I think the last time we walked out with Mr. and Mrs. Coddle, that you might have offered me your arm, and not have left me to the care of the husband, while you flirted with the wife.

Lynx. What do you call flirting?

Mrs. Ly. Whispering—laughing—and affecting to have, or really having, a quantity of interesting secrets. Don't ask me for a definition of the word, sir—I am not a dictionary.

Lynx. I think you are, my dear—if I may judge by the hard words that you ever use to me. Proceed with your charges, I beg.

Mrs. Ly. I heard of your being in a private box at the theatre two evenings since—and with some strange female.

Lynx. Your hearing such a report is no evidence of its truth.

Mrs. Ly. You were not at home on that evening; indeed, I don't know when you are at home; always out; always running about; calling on this lady, and meeting that; receiving notes of assignation, and—but I'll not endure it longer, Mr. Lynx—you may provoke me beyond the bounds of endurance, and then beware——

Lynx. Of what, dear?

Mrs. Ly. That is best known to myself.

Lynx. I am grateful for the information, (*rising*) and now having discussed a very conjugal breakfast, I shall prepare for my morning walk.

Mrs. Ly. Is it possible that you can have no particular appointment? Have you had neither pink nor blue note this morning?

Lynx. No, my love. (*a twopenny postman's knock heard*, L.)

Mrs. Ly. There's the postman.

Lynx. So I hear.

Mrs. Ly. A letter for you, no doubt. I thought it would be strange if a morning passed without the arrival of some mysterious billet for Mr. Lynx. (LYNX *makes a movement towards the* L. *entrance, but resumes his seat*) Oh, sir, don't check your impatience—anticipate your servant and run to the door, I beg.

Lynx. Certainly, my love—if you wish it.

(LYNX *jumps up, and runs off*, L.)

Mrs. Ly. Now, sir, I think I have you in my snare; 'tis my own letter that has arrived, bearing a fictitious signature, and appointing to meet him in the park alone. He will receive it, read it—then what should he do—what *should* a good and true husband do under such circumstances? Show the letter to his wife. Will he do that? If he does I will freely forgive—forget—and think all I have seen and heard to be delusions and false-hoods;—but if he neither gives it me, nor alludes to it in any way, I shall be convinced of his perfidy, and my course shall be resolved on.

Re-enter LYNX, *singing carelessly*, "I have pluck'd the fairest flower," *etc., etc.*

Lynx. By Jove, I must dress; 'tis near eleven. (*looking at his watch*) My love, I think I shall dine at my club to-day.

Mrs. Ly. Was the letter that you have just received an invitation to meet some one there?

Lynx. Oh, dear, no.

Mrs. Ly. Was it from any one that I am acquainted with?

Lynx. No, t'was merely a note.

Mrs. Ly. On a matter of business?

Lynx. Yes—yes—mere business.

Mrs. Ly. Which, of course, you will attend to?

Lynx. Business *must* be attended to, my dear.

Mrs. Ly. Especially when the only business of a man is pleasure.

Lynx. Precisely.

Mrs. Ly. Then you *are* going out ?

Lynx. I am.

Mrs. Ly. I think, on such a fine morning as this, you might for once take me with you.

Lynx. Certainly, my love, if you wish it.

Mrs. Ly. Ah ! will he take me ? *(aside)*

Lynx. Yet, now, I think if it,—I have two or three places to call at, where I may be detained.

Mrs. Ly. I can wait for you.

Lynx. That'll be so unpleasant ; I shall be fidgetty at the thoughts of your becoming impatient, and half the little matters that I may have to arrange may escape my memory. You had better name to-morrow for our walk.

Mrs. Ly. You *won't* take me this morning ?

Lynx. Not this morning.

Mrs. Ly. You *will* go out ?

Lynx. I must.

Mrs Ly. Very well, sir, *(aside)* Perfidious man, you will bitterly repent this treatment of me. (CODDLE *speaks outside*) there is some one in the hall.

Lynx. *(looking off* L.) They're your friends, Mr. and Mrs. Coddle, they will amuse you during the ten minutes that I require for dressing. What a strange couple—so oddly assorted, poor Coddle is the thinnest, chilliest man in the world. You must shut all your windows.

Mrs. Ly. His wife will immediately open them.

Lynx. She, poor thing, is so hot. When he is below freezing point, she is above fever heat.

Mrs Ly. You must allow that they do endeavor to accommodate themselves to each other's foibles, and not oppose them, and use them as the means of tormenting, as *some* people do !

Lynx. We shall see.

Enter MR. *and* MRS. CODDLE L., CODDLE *wrapped up in a great coat, over which is a spencer ; a boa round his throat ; a cravat covering his chin, and a Welsh wig on his head.* MRS. CODDLE *is dressed in thin white muslin.*

Cod. Ah, Mrs. Lynx !

Mrs. Cod. Good morning my friends.

Lynx. How d'ye do ? How d'ye do ?

Cod. I'm very cold—ugh ! *(shuddering)*

Lynx. Quite well, Mrs. Coddle ?

Mrs. Cod. Very well—but so hot. Phew ! Pray open the windows and give me some air.

Cod. No, don't, don't—I shall jump out of one of 'em, if you do. My inhuman wife would drag me from my warm fireside this morning, although I told her there was an incipient easterly wind fluttering about. If it should blow in full force before I get home, I shall die.

Mrs. Cod. My dear love—'tis nothing but a fine refreshing breeze, and one that you ought to be very grateful for.

Cod. I tell you it is warmth that I want—warmth.

Mrs. Cod. And it's air that I want—fine, fresh, blowing, whistling air.

Cod. (*shuddering*) Ugh—don't dear ; you chill me to the bone to hear you. ·

Lynx. Be seated, I beg. (*crosses to* L.) Excuse me for a few minutes. (**Exit** LYNX, L.)

Mrs. Ly. (*aside*) If he does go out, I'll follow him, watch him, and enjoy his disappointment.

Cod. You have a window open somewhere, Mrs. Lynx—pray shut it. I sat in a draught last week, that so completely fixed my head upon my shoulders, that I couldn't have moved it without turning my whole body at the same time, had it been to save my life.

Mrs. Cod. Merely a stiff neck, Mrs. Lynx.

Cod. All my wife's fault. I sat for five days in this attitude. (*holding his head up stiffly*) If I wanted to look at anybody on my left, I was obliged to turn my whole body thus. If any one spoke to me on my right, I could only attend to them by pivoting so. If I wished to see what was going on behind me, I was obliged to whirl round like a weathercock at a sudden change in the wind ; but how do you think I managed my movements ?

Mrs. Ly. I really can't guess.

Cod. 'Twas the only thing I could hit upon. I sat upon my wife's music-stool for five whole days. I ate, drank, lived and twirled upon a music-stool ;—all through sitting in a draught— do shut your windows, there's a dear.

Mrs. Cod. You'll suffocate me some day, Coddle—I know you will. You don't know what a life I lead with him, Mrs. Lynx— five blankets in July—think o' that.

Cod. Highly necessary—we are more liable to take cold in hot weather, than in any other. I always have four colds, one rheumatism, and two stiff necks every July.

Mrs. Cod. What d'ye think he did a week ago, Mrs. Lynx ? I had retired early ; in the middle of the night I awoke in such a state of alarm—I really thought the room beneath us was on fire the air of my apartment was so hot, so sultry, that I could not draw my breath ; I gasped for air. What can be the matter ? I said to myself. Surely, I've been suddenly transported to the Indies, and there is a thunderstorm brewing. I rose—I opened the windows——

Cod. And almost killed me on the spot ; there was a strong north wind blowing at that moment—enough to wither one—imprudent woman.

Mrs. Cod. 'Twas a fine bracing night breeze—but out of kindness to Coddle, I immediately closed the windows—Phew ! Oh, gracious, had you but have felt the heat—I fainted away in the easy-chair—Coddle rang the bell—the servants came—and, to my horror, we discovered that Coddle had clandestinely introduced a German-stove into the bedroom, and there it was red hot. Think what a person of my temperament must have endured ! I've been ill ever since.

Cod. Dr. Heavysides recommended it ; he said 'twas the only thing that could save my life, and rescue me from a threatened pulmonary complaint. I've had a wheezing cough ever since its removal—barbarous woman ! (*coughs*)

Mrs. Cod. You seem dull, Mrs. Lynx.

Mrs. Ly. I'm not in very good spirits.

Mrs. Cod. Ah ! we poor wives all have our little troubles.

Cod. And we poor husbands too. Mrs. Coddle won't let me wear a bear-skin comforter—did you ever hear of such cruelty !

Mrs. Cod. He thinks of nothing but his own personal ease.

Cod. I'm obliged ; there's no one else thinks of it for me.

Mrs. Cod. He's the most apathetic creature living—no life, no passion, no impulse. I *do* like to see a husband subject to some little caprices of temper. If Coddle, now, were inclined to jealousy—and would scold me well—and throw things about, and go into a fury now and then, I should be the happiest woman in the world ; but he won't—there he sits from morning till night, as carefully wrapped up as an Egyptian mummy, I really think he is one ; he is—he's King Cheops. (*aside to* Mrs. Lynx) Oh, Mrs. Lynx, I'd give the world to make him jealous. But what is the matter with you—have you had words with your husband ?

Mrs. Ly. I confess that we have had a trifling disagreement this morning.

Mrs. Cod. How delightful !—Coddle, why don't you go into a passion, and knock me down ?

Cod. My dear, if I were to go into a passion, and suddenly cool, as I know I should, the checking of the perspiration would be the death of me—I should die.

Re-enter Lynx, *dressed for walking.*

Lynx. Good morning, my friends ! I am going to leave you ; don't you hurry away on my account.

Mrs. Ly. There's no necessity for that ; I shall be alone the whole day.

Mrs. Cod. (*to* Mrs. Lynx) Ah ! you are a happy woman in possessing such a husband ! Look at him, Coddle ; observe his manner—his air. Why don't you dress in that fashion ?

Cod. Me ! as thinly clad as Mr. Lynx is now—would you see me in my grave ? Ugh ! I shudder to look at him.

Mrs. Cod. I'm sorry that you are going out. (*to* LYNX) I thought to have passed a very pleasant morning in your society.

Mrs. Ly. (*aside*) I'm certain there's an understanding between them. (*watching them with suspicion.*)

Mrs. Cod. (*to* LYNX) A word with you. (*she whispers to* LYNX, *and laughs.*) Ha ! ha ! ha ! it would be very droll, now —would it not ?

Lynx. Ha ! ha ! very, indeed.

Mrs. Cod. I shall endeavor——

Lynx. Do, do—rely upon me. Ha ! ha !

Mrs. Cod. Ha ! ha ! ha !

Lynx. Adieu, my friends, adieu. Good morning, Mrs. L. If I do not return by five, you need not expect me till late.—Adieu. (**Exit,** L.)

Mrs. Ly. May I ask, madam, why you whispered my husband ?

Mrs. Cod. A mere matter of pleasantry.

Mrs. Ly. Indeed !

Mrs. Cod. He's the most charming creature living, is that husband of yours. I wish my poor drone was like him.

Mrs. Ly. I should be sorry to make your husband unhappy, madam.

Mrs. Cod. Do, do—make him wretched, there's a love—but for once.

Mrs. Ly. I don't comprehend you, madam—I can only observe, that your conduct to my husband, a moment since, was as ill-mannered as it seemed suspicious.

Mrs. Cod. He's a fine spirited man. (*looking at* CODDLE, *who is busy wrapping himself closely up*)

Mrs. Ly. Indeed ! pray, madam, what might be the subject of your whispers ?

Mrs. Cod. I never betray confidences.

Mrs. Ly. Surely you are not that base woman, who, under the mask of friendship, seeks to ruin my peace ? I have watched your behavior before, madam, and I am now convinced there is some secret correspondence between you and my husband ; and how Mr. Coddle can sit there, and affect to be blind to your actions, I am at a loss to conceive.

Cod. Blind—I affect to be blind—what is there to see, madam ?

Mrs. Cod. (*aside*) This is delicious ;—if Coddle would but listen to her.

Mrs. Ly. What is there to see ?--quit my house, and from this moment I trust that neither of you will enter it again.

Cod. What have we done ?

Mrs. Ly. (*to* Mrs. Coddle) I look upon you, madam, as a dangerous woman.

Cod. So she is, my nightcaps are never thoroughly aired.

Mrs. Ly. And if your husband can countenance your conduct, I'm not so lost to every sense of self-respect as to submit to it.

Mrs. Cod. Bless me, Mrs. Lynx, what do you mean ?

Cod. (*coming between them*) Don't, don't, pray don't excite me ; if you get to words I must interfere, and any interference, at this moment, might be fatal.

Mrs. Ly. I shall not attempt to explain my insinuations—I only desire that you will leave me to myself, and that your visits here may be less frequent.

Mrs. Cod. Don't you stir from this house, Coddle, till you are perfectly convinced of the baseness of her innuendos. Be jealous, and demand an explanation ; if you don't, I'll tear the list from all the doors at home.

Mrs. Ly. Will you compel me to ring the bell ?

Mrs. Cod. Go into a rage, Mr. Coddle.

Cod. I can't (Mrs. Lynx *throws open a window*, R.) My love, we are in a thorough draught ; that woman wants to destroy me. Let us leave the house, if you wish to see me alive an hour hence. Be satisfied—I'll call on Mr. Lynx, and demand an explanation.

Mrs. Cod. But one word more——

Cod. No, no, not one. Come, my dear, I've the rheumatics in my right shoulder already—I tremble from head to foot—I've taken cold, and you'll have to nurse me for a month. Come, dear, come.   (**Exit** L., *dragging off* Mrs. Coddle.)

Mrs. Ly. (*falling into a chair*) Wretched woman that I am, why did I ever give power to any man so to torment me ? I'll now follow Mr. Lynx, and enjoy his disappointment.

Mrs. Cod. (*without*) Don't send up your name at present, the poor creature is in a rabid state.

Mrs. Y. (*heard without*) Mrs. Lynx won't mind us.

Mrs. Ly. (*looking off*, L.) Who is this ? Mr. and Mrs. Younghusband ?—how provoking—just as I'm going out. What can bring them here ?—they are a couple that I can't endure ; though married but three months, they are perpetually contradicting and annoying each other ; if, now, they had suffered the five years of matrimony that I have, there might be some excuse for them ; but to disagree so early in their career is sad indeed.

Enter MR. *and* MRS. YOUNGHUSBAND, L.

Mrs. Y. (*running to* Mrs Lynx, *and taking both her hands*) How do you do, dear ? don't mind me and Y., coming in so unceremoniously—we have called to give you some information.

Young. How can you talk so absurdly, Louisa? we have not called to give Mrs. Lynx any information.

Mrs. Y. For what, then?

Young. Merely to tell her that a person wishes to see her.

Mrs. Y. Well, *that* is information.

Young. No, it isn't.

Mrs. Y. Yes it is.

Young. How can that be?

Mrs. Y. To tell anybody of any matter, is to inform·them; and to inform people is, of course, to give them information. How you do contradict me!

Mrs. Ly. What then, is the information that you bring me?

Mrs. Y. There, you hear, sir, Mrs. Lynx allows it to be information.

Young. It can't be.

Mrs. Y. But it is.

Young. It isn't; you have not informed Mrs. Lynx of anything yet.

Mrs. Y. I should have done so, if you had not interrupted and contradicted me, as you always do.

Young. Allow me to tell Mrs. Lynx. You must know, madam, that some years ago, my wife was sent to the boarding-school of Mrs. Dove, in Sussex——

Mrs. Y. No, it was in Kent.

Young. In Sussex.

Mrs. Y. In Kent, I tell you.

Young. If you aggravate me in this manner, I'll go home again.

Mrs. Ly. Well—well.

Mrs. Y. Last night, at a friend's house, we accidentally met Mr. and Mrs. Dove—when she informed us that she had given up her school, and was now in London for the purpose of collecting some old debts, and amongst the names of the persons that she had to call on, was that of Mr. Lynx——

Mrs. Ly. My husband?

Mrs. Y. Your husband.

Young. Louisa, how can you? why will you thus agitate Mrs. Lynx? You are not sure the Mr. Lynx, that Mrs. Dove is looking for, is the husband of our friend; we merely surmised that it was.

Mrs. Y. I tell you, I'm certain it is the same.

Young. You are not.

Mrs. Y. I am.

Young. It can't be the same.

Mrs. Y. It is.

Young. It isn't.

Mrs. Ly. Now, pray don't trifle with me; think of my dreadful suspense; think of my feelings at this moment.

Mrs. Y. Mrs. Dove is now below, with her husband ; shall I ask her to walk up ?—then she can relate this strange circumstance herself.

Young. You ought first to tell Mrs. Lynx, who and what the people are, before you introduce them to her.

Mrs. Y. There is no necessity for it.

Young. There is.

Mrs. Y. There isn't.

Young. I tell you there is.

Mrs. Ly. Yes, yes—pray tell me.

Mrs. Y. Well, then—Mrs. Dove, you must know, was a widow, and formerly the mistress of a large boarding-school ; but has now retired, after marrying her footman. They are the oddest couple you ever met with. She is perpetually drilling her husband into politeness and correct pronunciation, which the poor man will never comprehend as long as he lives. Oh, had you but seen them last night ! Whenever a bell rang, poor Mr. Dove could scarcely help starting from his chair, and running to attend to it ; and could only be checked by the alarming eyes of Mrs. Dove. Ha ! ha !—Oh, those eyes—how they did remind me of my school-days ! just the looks that she used to dart at us poor refractory girls.

Young. My dear, why don't you keep to that portion of the narrative most interesting to Mrs. Lynx ; she don't want to hear of great eyes and refractory girls.

Mrs. Y. I am sure I have mentioned all that is necessary.

Young. You have not.

Mrs. Y. I have.

Young. You have not.

Mrs. Ly. Ask them to walk up, I shall then be satisfied.

Mrs. Y. (*calling*) Step up, Mrs. Dove, and bring your husband with you.

Young. There is no necessity for calling up Mr. Dove.

Mrs. Y. There is.

Young. There isn't.

Mrs. Y. There is.

Young. They are here ; don't make a noise.

Mrs. Y. 'Twas you that made the noise.

Young. 'Twas not.

Mrs. Y. It was.

Enter Mr. and Mrs. Dove, L.

Mrs. Y. Mrs. Lynx—Mr. and Mrs. Dove. Will you be kind enough to relate to Mrs. Lynx the purport of your inquiry ?

Mrs. Dove. The purport of my inquiry is to ascertain, whether the Mr. Lynx, that I am informed is residing here, is the identical person who, two years ago, placed a young lady under my care.

Mrs. Ly. A young lady! My husband place a young lady under your care?

Young. Nay, madam, before you distress yourself, you had better be assured that the Mr. Lynx alluded to *is* your husband.

Mrs. Dove. The gentleman's christian cognomen was Lionel.

Dove. Lionel Lynx, Esquire.

Mrs. Dove. Silence, my dear!

Dove. That is what was on the trunk he sent to our house; that's all I know, my precious.

Mrs. Ly. The name is perfectly correct.

Mrs. Dove. I was told that he had been in the army——

Mrs. Ly. Right, madam.

Mrs. Dove. But had sold his commission, and was married.

Mrs. Ly. You are right, madam—it is the same; there is not the slightest shadow of a doubt but 'tis the same ;—and this person that he placed with you, what was she?

Mrs. Dove. A young lady of great personal attractions.

Mrs. Ly. Ha!

Dove. She played the harp *diwinely*.

Mrs. Dove. Divinely, dear; think of your v's.

Dove. Hang them *we's ;* I shall never get over 'em.

Mrs. Dove. She was placed at my establishment, not so much with a view to education, as with reference to the meeting with a comfortable and respectable home at a moderate charge.

Dove. A hundred a year, and bring your own silver knife, fork, spoon, and six towels!

Mrs. Dove. Hush, love, we must forget the school now!

Mrs. Ly. I never heard of this. Who could the girl have been? What was her age?

Mrs. Dove. At that time, seventeen.

Mrs. Ly. Her name?

Mrs. Dove. Harriet Seymour.

Mrs. Ly. Where is she now?

Mrs. Dove. That question I am quite incompetent to answer —she resided with me a year and a half, and at the end of that time suddenly disappeared.

Dove. We think she eloped, for every now and then somebody used to come and sing under the window, to such a degree that all the girls in the house went raving mad.

Mrs. Dove. Silence, dear.

Dove. Yes, darling.

Mrs. Dove. At the time of the young lady's disappearance, there remained a small balance in my favor on her account, for extras, and of which I think it probable that Mr. Lynx is not aware.

Dove. Eight pound odd.

Mrs. Dove. Pounds, dear; speak in the plural.

Dove. Pounds, love.

Mrs. Ly. I'm in a maze—bewildered.   Who can this girl have been !   Did she—did she seem attached to him ?

Mrs. Dove. Very.

Dove. He called once, and I happened to enter the room quite promiscuously where they was—

Mrs. Dove. Where they were ; *I* was—they *were.*

Dove. Where they were ; and I saw the young lady a *dissolving* away into tears upon his shoulder.   I was then Mrs. Dove's footman.

Mrs. Dove. Henry !

Dove. Martha !

Mrs. Dove. How often have I told you never to touch——

Dove. Oh, la !   Ah, I forgot.

Mrs. Ly. T'was some victim of his villainy, no doubt.   How to discover the mystery—how to come upon him, when he may be unprepared for equivocation !   I have it, my friends.   (*to* MR. *and* MRS. YOUNGHUSBAND)   If you should meet Mr. Lynx, let me implore you not to breathe a syllable of this matter to him ; let me be the first to tell him.   Pray oblige me by dining here to-morrow.   (*to* MR. *and* MRS. DOVE)   You shall then be introduced to my husband ; and should he indeed be the person who placed that girl under your care, he cannot dare to deny it.   You, my friends, (*to* MR. *and* MRS. Y.) will also be here—nay, I will invite every soul that I am acquainted with, and publicly expose his villainy.

Mrs. Dove. We will do ourselves that honor.

Mrs. Ly. To-morrow, at five.

Mrs. Dove. We shall be punctual, madam.

Dove. (*aside to* MRS. D.) You said you'd take me to the *Jew-*ological Gardens.

Mrs. Dove. We must defer it, my dear.   (*aside to* DOVE.)

Dove. That's the way you always serve me ; you never promise to take me anywhere, but I am continually disapp'inted.

Mrs. Dove. Pointed !

Dove. Pointed.   You use me shameful, dear.

Mrs. Dove. Don't be an idiot, love.

Dove. You are a brute, precious.

Mrs. Dove. Henry !   (*looking fiercely at him*)

Dove. Oh, them eyes—I never can answer 'em.

Mrs. Dove. Then to-morrow at five, Mrs. Lynx.

Mrs. Ly. I shall rely on your being here—you will not disappoint me ?

Mrs. Dove. Certainly not.   Good morning, Madam.   Now, Henry, your arm ?

Mrs. Ly. The servant shall see you to the door.

MRS. LYNX *pulls a bell-rope hanging by the side of the fire-place ; a bell rings.* DOVE *suddenly starts, and is running confusedly as if to answer it, when* MRS. DOVE *checks him.*

Mrs. Dove. My lamb, you forget yourself.

Dove. Deuce take them bells, I never can hear one without running to answer it.

Mrs. Dove. Good morning, Mrs. Lynx ; good morning, madam; good morning, sir. (*curtesying profoundly to each*) Now, my dear, (*aside to* DOVE) don't forget to leave the room like a gentleman.

They approach the L. *door, when they both make a profound obeisance, and go off.* MRS. LYNX *falls in a chair, hiding her face in her hands.*

Mrs. Y. My dear Mrs. Lynx, pray don't allow this matter to affect you so seriously.

Young. Louisa, why do you check the feelings of our friend ? You ought to be aware that tears are a great relief when one is suffering from mental agitation.

Mrs. Y. No, they ain't ; a pretty relief, indeed, to break one's heart with crying.

Young. It is a relief.

Mrs. Y. No, it isn't—how do you know ?—you never cry, you hardened creature.

Young. I prefer preserving my tears for a certain event.

Mrs. Y. Ah ! when you lose *me ?*

Young. Yes, dear.

Mrs. Y. That's the kindest thing you have said since our marriage.

Young. No, it isn't.

Mrs. Y. Yes, it is.

Young. It isn't.

Mrs. Y. It is.

Mrs. Ly. My dear friends—pray cease your bickering.

Mrs. Y. He will always contradict me.

Mrs. Ly. If you meet my husband, pray be silent on this matter, and be here to-morrow, I beg ; and should I be compelled to take a desperate resource to conquer the feelings that now consume me, you will know how to pity and to pardon me. (*she sinks into a chair.*)

Mrs. Y. Come, Frederick, we'll leave poor Mrs. Lynx ; people don't like to have their sorrows intruded upon.

Young. We ought rather to stay and console her.

Mrs. Y. A charming consoler you are—how did you console me yesterday, when that frightful bonnet was sent home ?

Young. 'Twas your own taste.

Mrs. Y. It was not.

Young. You insisted upon having a fall of blonde in the front of it.

Mrs. Y. That is the thing I detest.

Young. It is the very thing that you ordered.

Mrs. Y. When I tried it on, you told me that I never looked so frightful in all my life.

Young. I didn't.

Mrs. Y. You did—I'll burn it when I go home.

Young. Indeed you shall not.

Mrs. Y. I will—and I'll wear my dirty yellow one to vex you.
(*Exit* L.)

Young. Louisa ! how can you be so absurd ? Louisa, why don't you wait for me ?—you're the most aggravating woman I ever met with.

Mrs. Y. (*without*) I shall go home alone.

Young. You shall not. (*rushing out* L.)

Mrs. Y. I will. (*without*)

Young. You shall not. (*without*)

Mrs. Y. I will.

Young. You shall not.

Mrs. Y. I hate you.

Young. You don't.

Mrs. Y. I do.

Young. You don't.

Mrs. Y. I do.

The voices of MR. *and* MRS. YOUNGHUSBAND *are heard contradicting each other, till they gradually cease.*

Mrs. Ly. I surely never felt the passion of jealousy, till this moment ; all my past suspicions have been mere faults of temper compared with the restlessness, the wretched thoughts, and sinking of the heart that I now endure. Who can this girl be ! Where is she now ? *He* knows full well—no doubt he visits her —may be at this moment in her society. I'll leave the house— him—all—for this agony is more than I can bear. (*she is rushing out* L., *when* LYNX *appears.*)

Lynx. Where are you going in such haste ?

Mrs. Ly. (*controlling her feelings*) So soon returned ?

Lynx. I had forgotten my purse. (*going to desk, on a table up the stage*)

Mrs. Ly. I hope you have been gratified by your walk.

Lynx. Yes, perfectly.

Mrs. Ly. Of course you were not so much annoyed at your disappointment, but you sought amends in some more certain amusement.

Lynx. Yes, dear,—I returned to you.

Mrs. Ly. You little thought that your note of assignation— your note of "mere business," was written by me.

Lynx. It was, eh ! And pray, what end has the paltry trick answered ?

Mrs. Ly. Your immediate attention to it has convinced me of your perfidy.

Lynx. Indeed ! Could you think of no better plan to convict me ? (*taking a chair*)

Mrs. Ly. I have little occasion to tax my invention further, sir ; I now feel quite assured of my misery.

Lynx. Of what misery ?

Mrs. Ly. The possession of a husband who practices conceal-ment. (*aside*) I did not intend to breathe a syllable of what I have heard ; but I cannot resist. I must tell him—perhaps he may be guiltless. Lionel ! is the name of Harriet Seymour known to you ?

Lynx. (*starting from his seat*) Who has dared to utter that name to you ? who has dared to breathe a word of that person ?

Mrs. Ly. Ha ! now I am, indeed, firmly—wretchedly con-vinced. What, sir ! your agitation leaves you defenceless ?—Where are your arts—your falsehoods—your equivocations, now ?

Lynx. Who has been here ?

Mrs. Ly. I shall not name.

Lynx. By heaven, you shall ! (*seizing her arm.*)

Mrs. Ly. Hold, sir ! would you use violence ? Would you conceal your shame by rage ? Listen to me ! Ere I quite decide upon my course, I will give you one opportunity of justifying yourself—one chance of a full and fair explanation. Promise me to be at home to-morrow,—I will not, in the mean time, allude to this matter, by a single word ; no, no—till then, I will conquer my feelings and be silent. I shall be sorry to proceed in the revenge that I contemplate ; but should I have cause—remember, 'twas your own hand that cast down the fire-brand here ; and if I do take it up, and set the home of our happiness in flames, you alone are to blame. (**Exit**, R.)

Lynx. What can she mean ? Does she threaten me with re-taliation ? Who can have been here—through what channel can she have heard ? But I must avoid all explanation ; I dare not reveal aught connected with that unhappy girl.

Enter CODDLE, L.

Cod. Excuse my coming in so unceremoniously—I knew you were here—I saw you come home—merely called to oblige Mrs. Coddle. There's that window still open ; permit me to shut it. (*he crosses to* R., *and pulls down the window*) Mrs. Lynx has hinted to my wife that a familiarity exists between you and her, and one that I ought not to shut my eyes to ; now, I candidly confess that I have opened them as wide as I can, and what Mrs.

Lynx can possibly mean, I am at a loss to guess. But entirely to oblige my wife, I call here, at the risk of my life—as I did not intend to come out any more to-day—to ask, if such a familiarity really exists ? Mrs. Coddle demands it, for my own satisfaction. If I am not satisfied, she insists on my fighting you ; and if I am satisfied she is determined to make Mrs. Lynx beg her pardon. Now what is to be done ?

Lynx. My dear sir, you well know the temper of my wife, and the pains that she takes to make herself wretched. Be assured that her suspicions are groundless.

Cod. I know they are ; and I am convinced it has all originated in my wife's anxiety to excite me.

Lynx. A word with you (*bringing* CODDLE *forward.*) I left you here when I went out this morning—did any one call during your stay ?

Cod. No one but Mr. and Mrs. Younghusband.

Lynx. (*aside*) Surely they can't have heard—no—no ; yet they may. Ha ! a thought strikes me. Sir, you have more than professed a friendship for me.

Cod. And have proved it, too. Didn't I visit you every week, when you lodged in that airy situation at Hampstead ?

Lynx. My wife has, by some means yet unknown to myself, discovered my connection with a young female.

Cod. Oh, you villain ! why don't you wear a Welsh wig ? you would escape all these troubles, then.

Lynx. I am compelled to avoid all explanation respecting her.

Cod. Well !

Lynx. 'Tis in your power to relieve me from my embarrassment.

Cod. In what way ?

Lynx. This young female, I, some time since, placed at a country school for protection——

Cod. You rogue !

Lynx. She disappeared, and all trace of her had been lost.

Cod. Well ?

Lynx. My wife has this moment mentioned her name.

Cod. Then, of course, she has discovered your trick ?

Lynx. You must publicly declare this girl to be your own.

Cod. What !

Lynx. Your own daughter—and that to save your secret, I undertook her charge.

Cod. Bless you ! what would Mrs. Coddle say ? My dear boy, she'd murder me. I could not support such an assertion for the world ; how could I ever look in my wife's face afterwards ?

Lynx. With more confidence than were she to know——

Cod. What ?

LYNX *whispers to* CODDLE, *who staggers back to a chair, in great alarm.*

Cod. I'm a dead man.

Lynx. I am in possession of more than you thought for, Mr. Coddle. Now, sir, you see the plot is not one of such very great difficulty to execute. If you will not assist me, I must proclaim——

Cod. Not a word, on your life—plunge me into a cold bath, make me sleep a whole night on the top of the Monument—compel me to do anything for which I have a horror—but breathe not a word of *that*—of *that*——

Lynx. Do then, as I request.

Cod. I will—I swear it—there—— (*falling on his knees.*)

Lynx. Save *my* secret, and I will preserve *yours*.

END OF ACT I.

———

ACT II.

Scene I.—*An apartment in the house of* MR. CODDLE. MRS. CODDLE *discovered at the table, a note in her hand.*

Mrs. Cod. How very odd ! how very strange ! though this note arrived last night, I have scarcely done anything since but read it. (*reads*) " My dear Mrs. Coddle, pray pardon the warmth of my temper, that led me to use certain expressions to you, of which, at the time, I was not conscious ; though now, on recollection of them, I express my sorrow. Forgive me, and dine with us at five to-morrow ; do not disappoint me on your life, as I have a strong reason for inviting you ; bring Coddle with you, of course. Sincerely yours, Emmeline Lynx." What a strange woman ! who would suppose, that yesterday, she desired me to quit the house and never enter there again. Well, I'm resolved to go. What a length of time Coddle takes for dressing ; 'tis now half-past four, and I have been ready this hour. (*she knocks at* R. D.) Coddle, you drone, make haste.

Cod. (*within*) I shall be ready immediately ; I am now putting on my fourth waistcoat.

Mrs. Cod. And he wears *six* ! How the man can exist in such a state I know not ; and what is the matter with him, I am equally at a loss to guess ; he has been overpowered with nervous agitation and in a high fever all the morning ; has been talking in his sleep all night. I could only catch the words " Don't—I'll say anything—declare anything—but don't." The man has something on his mind ; what can it be ! He surely can't have committed any crime—a robbery or a murder ? Oh the monster ! I must question him.

Enter CODDLE, R. D., *dressed for a dinner party.*
Well, my dear, are you better ?

Cod. Not much—I feel very faint.

Mrs. Cod. Give me your hand. (CODDLE *presents his hand timidly*) Dear—dear—what a burning fever you are in—your hands are like live coals ; and what a pulse ! (*feeling his pulse*) Heavens, Samuel !—you are ill.

Cod. I am.

Mrs. Cod. And the cause is not so much bodily infirmity as mental anxiety.

Cod. Lord !—do you—do you think so ?

Mrs. Cod. You are fainting ; let me open the windows.

Cod. No—no—not for worlds.

Mrs. Cod. What has caused this fever ?

Cod. I—I—don't know.

Mrs. Cod. Coddle, your mind is diseased.

Cod. My dear, don't speak to me in that fierce manner, you make me tremble from head to foot.

Mrs. Cod. You pass'd a wretched night.

Cod. I did.

Mrs. Cod. You talk'd in your sleep.

Cod. No ! (*alarmed*) Did I ; what did I say ?

Mrs. Cod. Sufficient to rouse my suspicions.

Cod. I have been criminating myself ; 'twas while I was dreaming of being hanged. (*aside*) What *will* become of me ?

Mrs. Cod. Tell me—what is this matter that has so suddenly disconcerted you ?

Cod. Ah !—she don't know—I breathe again.

Mrs. Cod. Answer me, sir ; what have you done ?

Cod. I—I—left off my life-preserving under-waistcoat, yesterday.

Mrs. Cod. Base equivocator—you shall have no rest, depend upon it, till I am perfectly acquainted with the cause of your agitation. I have watched your actions, sir, more than you are aware of ; 'tis something in which Mr. Lynx is concerned ; I observed you, when you returned from his house yesterday, you came home quite an altered man—you that were not to be roused by anything that did not interfere with your own immediate comfort, seemed suddenly to have changed your nature ; the servant left your room door open, unchecked ; a broken pane close to your ear escaped your notice ; you ate no supper ; you ordered no fire in your bedroom ; and your sleep was disturbed by sighs and groans, and words of guilt. Ha ! I have made you tremble : now, sir, I shall leave you, and in the meantime you will do well to prepare for a confession that I am resolved to wring from you. (*aside*) I have shaken him from his lethargy at last. **(Exit,** L.)

Cod. I am a lost man ; I knew my day of reckoning would arrive. Mary suspects something, that's clear—um !—and I'm going out to dinner, too. What a dinner it will be to me ; it must be a feast of poison, and a flow of woe ; if my secret is preserved, my promise to Lynx must lead to a commotion. Who can this girl be that I undertake to own ? ha ! ha !—now I think of it, I'm safe ; he *dare* not betray me ; he is as much in *my* power as I am in *his ;* yet how could he have discovered my unhappy situation ? He won't acknowledge that. No, no ; he considers that mystery adds to his stronghold upon me. I have borrowed a book of criminal jurisprudence from my attorney. I want to learn the utmost penalty of the law for my offence. (*he takes a book from his pocket, and turns over the leaves*) Here it is—bigamy ! (*reads*) " If guilty,"—what ? " *transportation* for life* " Oh ! (*falling in a chair*) Think of my being at Botany Bay—working night and day—summer and winter ; in trousers without lining ; only a shirt on my back ; and a chain round my leg ; no umbrella to put up when it rains ; no such thing as a yard of Welch flannel within a thousand miles of me, and nothing aired for me ; I should die ; the first damp night would send me to the tomb of the Coddles—oh ! (*shuddering.*)

Re-enter MRS. CODDLE, L., *introducing* MR. *and* MRS. DISMAL.

Mrs. Cod. Come in, come in ; there's nobody here but Coddle.
Cod. Ah, Mr. Dismal !—I was thinking of you.
Mrs. Cod. Mr. and Mrs. D. have also received an invitation to dine at Lynx's to-day ; and have called, in passing, to know if we were going.
Mrs. Dis. How ill poor Mr. Coddle looks !
Dis. What is the matter with him ?
Mrs. Cod. I'm sure I can't tell ; he keeps the cause of his illness a profound secret.
Mrs. Dis. He's like me ; he loves to pine in solitude, and brood over unrevealed sorrows.
Dis. You love to be a fool.
Mrs. Cod. Our friends are as much surprised at receiving an invitation from Mrs. Lynx as we were.
Mrs. Dis. For the last time we called there the poor woman thought proper to be jealous of *me.*
Dis. There was only that wanting to prove her madness.
Mrs. Dis. But she has a cause for her jealousy
Dis. Certainly, when you are present.
Mrs. Dis. Didn't we see him, yesterday, following a young person past our house ?
Dis. What of that ? 'tis a natural impulse to which our sex are peculiarly subject.

Mrs. Cod. Except Mr. Coddle—Were Venus herself to rise from the sea before him, he'd take to his heels for fear of catching cold from the foam.

Mrs. Dis. Tell Mr. Coddle the strange result of our inquiries, respecting Mr. Lynx's conduct.

Dis. Pooh! tell him yourself.

Mrs. Dis. The young person that we saw Mr. Lynx following, and striving to speak to, was joined by an elderly lady in black.

Cod. Eh! an elderly lady in black—'twas she, he told me she was in black.   (*aside.*)

Mrs. Dis. Of a very masculine appearance; Mr. Lynx seemed to enter into earnest conversation with her; when they parted, the two ladies entered a boarding-house, next door to us; our servant, gossiping with the footman, there, ascertained that the elderly lady in black—

Cod. Well——

Mrs. Dis. Had just arrived from Antigua——

Mrs. Cod. Where your property is situated.   (*to* CODDLE.)

Mrs. Dis. That she had taken lodgings, there for a short time; her object being to discover her husband, who had left her in the West Indies, and whose name, strange to say, was——

Cod. Oh!

CODDLE *has started up during* MRS. D'S *narrative, and is regarding her with intense curiosity, now falls back into his chair.*

Mrs. Cod. What's the matter!—what's the matter?

Dis. He has fainted.

Mrs. Dis. Here, here are my salts.

Dis. Open the windows—open the windows.

Mrs. Cod. No, no, you will kill him if you do.

DISMAL *makes to the windows, but is checked by* MRS. CODDLE; CODDLE, *on hearing that the windows are to be opened, is about to start from his chair, but checks himself, and resumes his position.*

Mrs. Dis. Get him some water—ring the bell.

Mrs. Cod. Stay, stay, I'll go myself.

MRS. CODDLE *runs off* R. 1 E.; CODDLE *suddenly starts up between* MR. *and* MRS. DISMAL, *and takes a hand of each.*

Cod. As you love me—if you do not wish to see me lifeless at your feet, breathe not a syllable relative to the elderly lady in black; mention not her name.

Dis. 'Twas your own.

Cod. I know it, I know it—'tis a terrible secret; a story of horror and despair; when we are alone, you shall know all; but not a word now, I beg—I implore—I pray—ah, my wife!

(*he falls back again into his chair.*)

Re-enter MRS. CODDLE *with a glass of water.*

Mrs. Dis. He's better now.

Dis. Much better.

Cod. (*affecting to revive*) Considerably better.

Mrs. Cod. I don't wonder at your fainting ; my only surprise is, that you can breathe at all in such an atmosphere ; there's not a breath of air permitted to enter the room. Phew ! I'm stifled ; excuse me a moment, my friends, I wish to speak to Coddle alone. (DISMAL *and his wife are going*) No, no—don't leave the room.

Cod. (*aside*) What can she be going to say ?

Mrs. Cod. Samuel !

Cod. My love !

Mrs. Cod. Surely your agitation, and your sudden faintness cannot arise from any apprehension.

Cod. Of what ?

Mrs. Cod. That this elderly lady in black, is——

Cod. No, no, no—oh, dear ! no, no !

Mrs. Cod. You anticipate me—not what ?

Cod. Not—I don't know. What were you going to say ?

Mrs. Cod. I have very strange and very terrible suspicions— 'tis surely no poor creature that you, in the hey-day of your youth——

Cod. No, no, no—my dear ! How can you think—how can you dream of such a thing ! I never had any hey-day—never ; don't think that of me. Come, come—let us go to Lynx's to dinner. Get ready, dear, get ready.

Mrs. Cod. I strongly suspect you.

MRS. CODDLE *goes up the stage, and throws a shawl on her shoulders.*

Cod. What will become of me ? If I escape the imputation of bigamy, the subject of that girl will be sufficient to bring my wife's vengeance on my head. I'll run and drown myself in a warm bath. I'll—no, no—I must rouse, I must rouse ; I must summon all my courage—all my fortitude—and bring out what little of the devil I have left in me.

Mrs. Cod. Now, Coddle, I'm quite ready.

Cod. So am I. (*putting on his hat*) Come along, I shall be very gay to-day ; you will wonder what possesses me. I shall be so gay ; come, Mrs. Dismal, take my arm, my dear, 'tis bad taste to walk with one's wife. D., look to Mrs. Coddle !

Mrs. Cod. The man's mad——

Dis. Raving.

Cod. You shall see me to advantage to-day ; I feel a new man, you may open all the doors and windows in the house. I'll do anything desperate to-day, walk to Lynx's without my coat, hat, anything—come, my love.—Come, Dismal—Fol de rol, de rol lol. (CODDLE *dances off with* MRS. DISMAL, L.)

Mrs. Cod. Mad !

Dis. Gone, quite gone. (**Exeunt,** *following.*)

Scene II.—*A Room at* LYNX'S.

Enter MRS. LYNX, R.

Mrs. Ly. The time has almost arrived that will either relieve me from the dreadful suspense that I now endure, or plunge me still deeper into misery ; since yesterday I have scarcely uttered a word in his presence ; I have religiously adhered to the resolution that I would not touch upon a subject that has so filled me with conflicting emotions ; but to-day, in an hour, I shall know the worst ; and if he be the guilty one that I am madly certain he is, his friends and the world shall know how I have been wronged, and for what purpose I have assembled them here. (*produces a letter*) Were it not for tokens like these, I should almost think that I had ceased to charm—had ceased to be looked upon even with interest, by the meanest of earth's creatures ; here is one that tells me he loves me ; my husband once told me so, but then I was younger and had a free heart to give ; that now, alas, is gone forever ; here is one who offers me wealth—splendor and affection —if I will forsake a husband that slights me—that torments and maddens me—what shall I do ? I have now the means of revenge —of a full and bold revenge. Shall I use them but to awe my husband, or shall I listen, and so make him rue the day that he first roused my jealousy ? But he may not be guilty—this girl may have no claim on him—beyond one of compassion or kindness. I may have suspected wrongly, and he may still have a lingering love for me, that may one day revive in all its early strength ; and then, were I to know him innocent, and myself the only guilty one, I should go mad—should die—should—oh, heaven, help me !

She falls, exhausted by her feelings, in a chair ; MR. *and* MRS. DOVE *heard* L.

Mrs. Dove. Now, my dear Henry, mind your behavior.

Mrs. Ly. Ah ! those people have arrived ; my husband has neither seen them, nor heard of their having been here. I shall watch him well when they first meet.

Enter MR. *and* MRS. DOVE, L.

Mrs. Dove. Good day to you, madam—I hope you find yourself in perfect health ?

Dove. (*bowing*) Good day, madam, feel yourself pretty well ?

Mrs. Dove. Henry, my dear, silence.

Mrs. Ly. I am obliged to you for being so faithful to your promise.

Mrs. Dove. 'Tis the height of ill-manners to disappoint one's friends in an *invite* to dinner.

Dove. And very stupid too, to refuse *wittles*.

Mrs. Dove. Henry, my dear——

Dove. My darling, you never will let me talk.

Mrs. Dove. Not till you know how, my love.

Dove. But my dear, if you don't let me practise, how am I ever to *in*quire the art ?

Mrs. Dove. *Ac*quire, verb active, to gain ; *in*quire, verb neuter, to ask questions ; acquire the art.

Dove. Acquire the *hart ?*

Mrs. Dove. Don't aspirate, love.

Dove. Oh, bother, dear.

Mrs. Ly. Let me beg of you not to allude to this young person till after dinner, I will then lead the conversation to that subject ; and then I hope you will freely and truly state all that you may know respecting her.

Enter LYNX, R.

Lynx. Emmeline, I—(*seeing* DOVE *and his wife*) What ! the mystery is now clear, that woman has traced me, has told my wife, but my secret is safe.

Mrs. Dove. Ah, Mr. Lynx, how d'ye do ? surprised to see me here no doubt ?

Lynx. No, madam, no.

Mrs. Dove. 'Tis some time since we met.

Lynx. Almost a year, I think.

Dove. Eleven months ! I ought to know, because we warn't united when Mr. Lynx used to give me half a crown for——

Mrs. Dove. Henry——

Mrs. Ly. I was informed that you knew these good people. (*to* LYNX.)

Lynx. Oh yes, my dear, they are my very old friends.

Mrs. Ly. Then I am happy in being the cause of renewing a friendship that seems so warm on either side ; come Mr. Dove, lead me to the dining-room, our friends have arrived, no doubt. Mr. Dove, will you favor me with your arm ?

Dove. Eh ! (*looking confused at his wife*) What am I to do ?

Mrs. Dove. Give Mrs. Lynx your arm.

Mrs. Ly. Lionel, will you bring Mrs. Dove ?

Lynx. (*offering his arm to* MRS. DOVE) Certainly.

Dove. (*leading off* MRS. LYNX, L.)Well, I declare, this *is* genteel life.

Mrs. Dove. Thank you, sir, you are very kind.

LYNX *leads off* MRS. DOVE, L. ; CODDLE *looks on*, R., *quite pale.*

Cod. I have been running all over the house to look for Lynx, —I thought I heard his voice here—how I tremble ! he must know that Mr. and Mrs. Dismal have seen that wretched woman— though they have promised secrecy, yet I cannot expect they will be always silent.

Re-enter LYNX, L.

Oh, my friend ! I have been looking for you—they are all at dinner, but I can't eat in the state of mind I am in. Mr. and Mrs. Dismal saw you talking to her.

Lynx. To whom ?

Cod. The elderly lady in black.

Lynx. They did !

Cod. Don't—don't look so astonished, you frighten me.

Lynx. They surely will not talk of it ?

Cod. They have promised to be secret, but what will be my feelings, in their presence !—when either of them speaks, I shall die with apprehension.

Lynx. Leave it to me ; we will see this woman to-morrow, and make some arrangement with her.

Cod. I'll say anything—do anything—give anything—only conceal the affair from my wife.

Lynx. Depend upon me, and be at peace. But be sure you do not equivocate in the question of this girl. The school-mistress with whom she lived is now here—at my very table. Remember ! I, at your request placed the girl under her care.

Cod. Yes.

Lynx. Because you did not dare confess to your wife that you had incurred such a responsibility,—but now you are anxious to acknowledge her.

Cod. What will Mary say ?

Lynx. Remember, you have sworn it.

Cod. I have, but tell me—who is this girl ?

Lynx. That is a mystery that I dare not disclose, even to you.

Cod. Bless me ! what two reprobates we are.

Lynx. Come to the drawing-room, I must make some excuse for your leaving the table. Now, be bold.

Cod. Yes, yes.

Lynx. Do not equivocate.

Cod. No, no.

Lynx. On your moral courage depends your own safety, and my happiness.

Cod. I know it, I know it.

Lynx. And the least appearance of timidity may ruin us ; now are you ready ?

Cod. Wait a moment. (*buttoning his coat up to his throat with great resolution*)

When I expect to be excited, I like to be guarded against taking cold—against the effects of draughts and currents of air. My courage is rising—it's up—now I'm ready—give me your arm— there, look at me ! Did you ever see a finer illustration of desperate courage ? Never.—Now to the field of action—to mortal strife—and death or victory.

(**Exit**, *dragging off* LYNX, L.)

Scene III.—*A drawing-room. All the party are discovered,* CODDLE *occupies the* R. *corner, in an easy chair ;* MRS. LYNX *is seated beside him ; next to her is* MR. YOUNGHUSBAND *and* MR. DISMAL ; MRS. DOVE *and* MR. LYNX *sit together,* MRS. DISMAL *next to him ; then* MRS. CODDLE *and* MRS. YOUNG-HUSBAND ; MR. DOVE *occupies the* L. *corner.*

All. (*but* CODDLE *and* LYNX) Astonishing ! to keep the matter a secret so long. Strange ! strange !

Lynx. Now, let us drop the subject. Mrs. Coddle, I trust that you will not respect or love your husband the less for this late disclosure ?

Mrs. Cod. Oh, no, no ; I merely feel hurt that he should have thought it necessary to have concealed the circumstance. Had I been a violent, jealous, bad-tempered woman, there might have been some cause for secresy ; but as everybody knows what a kind, indulgent creature I really am, he might have made me his confidant, and the poor girl should have been brought home. Where is she now ?

Lynx. Quite safe, depend upon it ; I will explain all at another opportunity.

Mrs. Ly. (*aside*) Falsehood, all falsehood, I'm convinced !

Lynx. (*to his wife*) Now, my dear, I trust you are perfectly satisfied ; and in this instance, I hope, you will confess that you were in error.

Mrs. Ly. Certainly, as I have no opposing evidence of the veracity of your story ; though, still, I think it very—very strange, that you should have so troubled yourself on Mr. Coddle's account ; if 'twere a mere act of friendship, the most famed heroes of antiquity have been surpassed.

Cod. Ha ! ha ! now I feel happy ; now my mind is at ease, and I'll be comfortable. How that Mrs. Dismal fixes her eyes on me ! Now fill your glasses ; Mr. Dove, take care of your lady.

Dove. Yes, yes. (*a knock and ring heard.*)

Lynx. Some arrival. (DOVE *jumps up, and runs off,* L.)

Mrs. Dove. (*starting up*) Henry, come back. I declare the man has gone to the door. Henry !

DOVE re-enters, L.

Dove. The door is opened ; there's an individual——

Mrs. Dove. Sit down, my dear, sit down.

Dove. (*aside*) I never shall get over answering the door when a knock comes. (*voices heard without in altercation.*)

A voice. You mistake ; you do, indeed ! You mistake.

Cod. (*apprehensively*) What is it ?

Dove. An individual——

Mrs Dove. Silence, Henry !

Mrs. Ly. (*rising*) The servant is in altercation with some one at the door ; who can it be ?

Lynx. (*rising*) Ring the bell.

Mrs. Ly. No, no, I'll go myself.

Cod. I have a horrid presentiment of evil ; a moment since I was glowing like a furnace, with joy ; and now I freeze again with terror.

Mrs. Cod. What's the matter, dear, do you feel cold ?

Cod. Yes—yes, ugh ! (*shuddering*)

Mrs. Cod. And I'm dying for air.

Mrs. Y. So am I, Mrs. Coddle.

Young. I am sure you are not.

Mrs. Y. I am.

Dismal. Shall I open the folding doors ?

Cod. No—no !

Dove. I feel very *languishing.*

Mrs. Dove. Henry ! *languid.*

Dove. Languid !—how she does take me up before people. (*aside*)

Cod. Hush ! here's Mrs. Lynx.

MRS. LYNX re-enters, *a letter in her hand.* CODDLE *regards her with anxiety.* MRS. LYNX *is trembling with agitation.*

Mrs. Ly. It was—it was as I suspected, a black falsehood.

Lynx. What is the matter ?

Cod. I shall fall flat on the floor, something is going to happen.

Mrs. Ly. `(*to* LYNX) Restrain your curiosity, sir ; you will know all in a moment ; there is a lady below.

Cod. I thought so.

Mrs. Ly. An elderly lady in black.

Cod. I'm a dead man. (*falling back in his chair, in utter despair*)

Mrs. Ly. She tells me that her name is Coddle——

Mrs. Cod. (*starting up*) What !

Mrs. Ly. (*pointing to* CODDLE) And that she is that man's wife.

Cod. (*groaning*) Oh ! I wish I could vanish through the floor.

Mrs. Ly. This letter is for you, madam.

Mrs. Cod. For me ! (*she tears the letter open, a marriage certificate falls on the floor*) What is this ? Oh, I can't read it

—I shall faint—I have no power to read ; pray take it, some one —Mr.—anybody—pray read it. (*she holds out the letter*, DOVE *takes it*)

All. (*but* CODDLE *and* MRS. DOVE) Read it, Mr. Dove.

Dove. I—I can't read.

Mrs. Dove. Henry—How can you so expose yourself ?

Dove. You read it, ma'am. (*giving it to* MRS. YOUNGHUSBAND)

Mrs. Y. Shall I read it, Mrs. Coddle ?

Mrs. Cod. Yes, yes, aloud—aloud—let the whole world hear it.

Mrs. Y. (*reading*) " Madam, the writer of this is an injured woman. The monster——

Cod. That's me—oh—

Mrs. Y. " The monster to whom you are married has another wife. I am that person ; the enclosed is a copy of my marriage certificate ; 'tis dated twenty years back. My object in coming to England is to claim a maintenance, and expose the villain.

" Your obedient servant,

" Belvidera Coddle."

All. Bless me ! Dear, dear, dear ! What a wretch—what a monster !

Mrs. Ly. The poor woman had better be asked up.

Cod. (*springing from his chair*) No, no ! I'd sooner face a thousand fiends than look once 'again on that dreadful being. My dear, my love ! (*to his wife*) You don't know what I have suffered—what I have endured, through that woman ! In the first place, I was decoyed—trapped. She left me. I once thought she was dead ; but——

Mrs. Cod. (*rising with dignity*) Silence, Samuel ! You have deceived me. I could have pardoned anything but this. As to the subject of the poor girl, that you have stated belongs to you, that I freely forgave.

Mrs. Ly. (*violently*) 'Tis false, Mrs. Coddle ! I asked the question of the bearer of that letter. I thought that she might be the parent of the girl ; but no, no ; your husband has but supported mine in a falsehood ; he never had a daughter. And you, sir, (*to* LYNX) are discovered and laid bare ; but I shall leave you this day, forever.

All. Nay, nay.

Mrs. Cod. And I shall quit *my* wretch. (*she advances to* CODDLE, *who buries his face in his hands*) From this moment, sir, we separate. Go to your wife, the woman who lawfully claims you, and never look me in the face again. We were an ill-assorted pair from the first ; but your affected apathy is now accounted for ; it arose from an evil conscience. Cold-hearted, deliberate deceiver ! farewell forever ! (MRS. CODDLE *rushes out*, L.)

Cod. Mary, come back ; come back ; hear me. (*he runs to* *the* L., *but suddenly stops*) I dare not follow her ; I shall meet the other. No, no ; I must fly ; I must leave the country ; 'tis now no home for me.

Lynx. Sit still, my friend ; be composed.

Cod. I can't ; I'll leave the house ; I'll——Ah, this door— (*pointing* R.)—leads to the canal ; I'll drown myself ; I'm desperate enough ; the sun has been on the water all day, so I've nothing to fear ; I am resolved upon my course—*felo-de-se,* nothing else. Adieu, my friends ; I'm a discovered, a guilty monster ; and this is the last time that you will ever see the distracted, wretched, Samuel Coddle. (CODDLE *rushes off* R.)

Young. (*starting up*) The man will drown himself.

Mrs. Y. No he won't ; sit still ; you'll only make matters worse.

Dis. Sit still all of you ; I know him ; when he comes in sight of the water, his courage will cool ; sit still.

Mrs. Dove. Shall my dear Dove follow him ?

Dove. I can't swim, duck !

Dis. No, no ; sit still.

Mrs. Ly. (*who has kept her eyes fixed on her husband throughout the scene*) What, sir ; not a word ? *quite* confounded ?

Lynx. Emmeline ! (*rising*) Appearances, I confess, are against me ; but you know not all. You know not the cause which compels me to this course ; be patient.

Mrs. Ly. I have been patient long enough, and will endure no more ; this is the last moment that I pass under your roof.

Lynx. Are you mad ? will you hear me ?

Mrs. Ly. No, sir.

Lynx. If you once quit the house, we never meet again.

Mrs. Ly. That is my wish.

Lynx. Be warned ;—if you leave me now—it *must*—it *shall* be forever.

Mrs. Ly. It is, sir, forever. (*rushes out,* L.—*all the company rise*)

Lynx. Nay, nay, keep your seats, my friends ; keep your seats. I will not have a soul stir a foot to expostulate with her ; let her take her own course. I have been in error, I confess ; but not to the extent that she supposes ; her causeless jealousies—her unceasing suspicions have wearied me, and she is free to go ; pray do not be disturbed on my account ; make yourselves happy ; I am sorry that our meeting should have ended thus ; but my wife is to blame ; she would not hear—would not listen to me ; and now. (*aside*) I leave this house, never to return. (**Exit,** R.)

Dove. Now he's gone ; shall I follow him, love ?

Mrs. Dove. No, no ; sit still, dear.

Mrs. Y. Call him back ! Mr. Lynx ! (*calling*) he'll do himself a mischief—I know he will.

Young. He won't ; sit still ; if you follow and torment him as you do me sometimes, you will, indeed, drive him to desperation.

Mrs. Y. *I* follow and torment you, sir ?

Young. You do—often—often.

Mrs. Y. You're an aggravating man, and——

Mrs. Dove. (*rising*) Nay, nay ; dear, dear ; pray don't get to words—my darling, Henry, hand that lady some wine ; sit still, there's a dear. (*to* MRS. YOUNGHUSBAND) Emulate Mr. Dove and me, we never utter a cross word to each other—do we, dear ?

Dov. No, love.   (*handing wine to* MRS. YOUNGHUSBAND.)

Mrs. Y. Take it away, sir, I don't want wine. Oh, sir, you need not sit there looking so fierce. (*to* YOUNGHUSBAND.) I was certain we should have a disagreement before the day was out ; you contradicted me about my silver thimble—you insisted that aunt Sarah gave it me.

Young. So she did.

Mrs. Y. She didn't—'twas uncle Tolloday gave it me.

Young. 'Twas aunt Sarah.

Mrs. Y. Uncle Tolloday.

Young. You're a provoking woman.

Mrs. Y. You're a hideous man.

Young. I'm going home.

Mrs. Y. I am not. I shall never go home any more.

Young. That won't break my heart.

Mrs. Y. *Your* heart ! you never had one.

Young. I had once.

Mrs. Y. Never.

Young. You drive me to madness ! I shall go home ; and I can only tell you, madam, since you threaten me, that when *you* arrive there you will receive no welcome from me.

Mrs. Y. Do you mean that ?

Young. I do.   (*he rushes off*, R.)

Mrs. Y. Then I'll go to my aunt Sarah ;—he shall never see me again, the aggravating creature. How I could ever marry him, I can't think ! It was uncle Tolloday that gave me the silver thimble—I know it was ; but he *will* contradict me. He does it on purpose to vex me—and oppose me—and worry me—and break my heart ; but I'll go this moment to my aunt's, and I'll never—never set foot in his house again.   (**Exit,** L.)

Mrs. Dove. Dear, dear ! what wretched lives some people do lead, don't they, love.

Dove. Yes, dear.

Mrs. Dis. (*to* DISMAL.) Just like you brutes of men—it's quite heart-breaking to see how we poor creatures are treated !

Dis. What is it to you ; nobody ill-treats you.

Mrs. Dis. *You* do ; I've been sitting here for this hour, and you have never spoken a word to me.

Dis. I had nothing to say.

Mrs. Dis. And though you know how fond I am of the wing of a fowl, you would send me a leg at dinner.

Dis. You women always want the wing.

Mrs. Dis. I'm a wretched woman.

Mrs. Dove. My dear Henry, can't you console poor Mrs. Dismal ?

Dove. Oh yes, love ! have a hapricot, ma'am ?

Mrs. Dove. *An* apricot—Henry, dear, you misapply your indefinite article.

Dove. Do I ?—console the lady yourself, love.

Mrs. Dis. The fact is—I had no business to marry you.

Dis. Now you speak the truth, we both ought to have known better ; when people have lived single for fifty years, they should learn to look on matrimony as a misery they have luckily escaped.

Mrs. Dis. You need not allude to my age, sir, before people.

Dis. What does it matter ? who cares how old you are ? you're fifty odd—so am I ; and we have been married a year and a half —more fool I—more fool you.

Mrs. Dis. (*crosses*, L.) I'm going home.

Dis. Well, go.

Mrs. Dis. Don't you intend to come with me !

Dis. No.

Mrs. Dis. You're an unkind man, and if we never meet again —I sha'n't be sorry.

Dis. Then the gratification will be mutual.

Mrs. Dis. Indeed ! I shall take you at your word, sir, (*going*) but, remember all my property is settled on myself.   (*Exit,* L.)

Dis. Serves me right—after living a bachelor fifty years, I had no right to alter my situation, but I'll apply for a divorce—I will —'twill be granted too ; I've an excellent plea—mutual insanity.
(*Exit,* R.)

Dove. Well—now all the people have gone, I've something to say—and something that I mean, too ; I won't be taken up, as I always am, before people.

Mrs. Dove. What do you mean, Henry, by being taken up ?

Dove. Why—altering my pronunciation every minute, as you do.

Mrs. Dove. How can I calmly sit and hear my husband commit himself in every syllable that he utters ? respect for you and for myself, renders it necessary that I should correct you.

Dove. Well, I don't like it—and I warn you not to *result* me again.

Mrs. Dove. *Insult* you.

Dove. Well, insult me again—you know how *wiolent* I am when I'm *exaggerated*.

Mrs. Dove. When you're exasperated.

Dove. Well, what's it matter ! you perfectly compromise my meaning.

Mrs. Dove. Henry—Henry—I will not hear you make use of such language. Had I been aware that you were so illiterate— I would have broken my heart ere I would have married you——

Dove. Yes—you never used to find fault with my language when we used to sit under the apple-tree of an evening.

Mrs. Dove. That I should not have seen the absurdity of uniting myself with one so opposite to me !

Dove. Opposite to you !—you never would let me be opposite to you, you was never easy but when I was by your side ; you know you wasn't.

Mrs. Dove. But love is blind——

Dove. Yes, and deaf too, if I may judge from my own situation ; just as if you couldn't have found out my pronunciation then as well as now.' I know'd there was a great *contract* between us.

Mrs. Dove. Contrast ! besides, you are so stupid ; you could not during dinner, hear a bell or a knock at the door, but you must be running to answer it. I sat on thorns for you.

Dove. Well, then, that was werry kind of you. I wouldn't do such a thing for my father ; but don't call me stupid—if you talk of bad language, what's that, I wonder ? Good-bye !—you won't see me again, in a hurry.

Mrs. Dove. Where are you going ?

Dove. I don't know where I am going, nor I don't care ; you've wounded me in a tender *pint.*

Mrs. Dove. Point !——

Dove. Point ! and I do not care if I never see you again.

Mrs. Dove. (*taking his hand*) Henry !

Dove. Let go my hand, Martha ; I mean what I say ; and don't follow me, because I won't be follow'd.

Mrs. Dove. You cannot intend to be so base ?

Dove. I do—you've put me in a passion, and when I am in a passion I'm *dissolute.* (**Exit,** R.)

Mrs. Dove. Resolute ! (*calling after him*) Cruel Henry ! I shall faint—Help ! Henry !—Water ! oh ! oh !

(*she faints in a chair and the drop falls.*)

END OF ACT II.

ACT III.

Scene I—*A meanly furnished room. A knock heard at* L. D. ; *after a pause,* CODDLE *peeps out of the door in flat.*

Cod. Who can that be ? I told the woman of the house on no account to admit a soul, or to tell any one who had taken her rooms ; but if she should be obliged to confess, to give out that a half-crazy gentleman occupies them, who will not allow a creature to approach him but herself. I think I am safe here, nobody knows me ; I've changed my name, I have paid a month's rent in advance, have closed and fastened the shutters and door, and intend to live in future by candle-light ; so here I am alone (*sitting in a chair*) with two wives claiming me, yet alone, that's something. What a night I have passed ! One minute trembling with apprehension, the next with cold ; the loose windows rattling all night like the chain of a sleepless felon—nothing but draughts all over the room, and a corner house too, its edges worn away by the wind constantly whistling round it—ugh ! (*shuddering—a knocking heard,* L. D.) It must have been the landlady that knocked ; she thought I was asleep, no doubt, so wouldn't disturb me ; how cold I am—there is a terrible wind somewhere. This is the most miserable place l ever was in, in my life ; where can that rush of air come from ! I must find out, here's my tow, (*going to table*) with this and a skewer, I can stop every crevice.

> *He goes round the room with a lighted candle ; he holds it before a crevice in the flat ; the flame of the candle waves.*

Ah ! here's the place, a thorough draught, enough to kill me. (*the candle goes out*) It has blown the candle out ; what a horrid place !

> *He hammers some tow into the crevice ; while thus employed, a knocking is again heard at the* L. D. ; CODDLE *starts, the hammer falls from his hand.*

Who's there ? 'tis the footstep of a man, it is not the landlady ; (*he creeps to the* L. D., *and listens*) officers of justice, perhaps, who dogged me here,—hush !

> *Listens again ; a loud knock makes him start away from the door.*

Shall I answer ? I will—I must—this suspense will drive me mad Who—who's there ?

Lynx. (*without*) My dear fellow, open the door.

Cod. Oh, it's my excellent friend, Lynx.

(*he runs to the door and unbolts it.*)
Come in, come in, quick, quick.

LYNX **enters** *;* CODDLE *immediately closes the door again, and bolts it.*

Now, what's the matter? how did you find me out? what brought you here? any of the police after me? any warrant granted? Speak, speak.

Lynx. No, no, calm your fears.

Cod. Was it you that knocked at the door a few minutes ago?

Lynx. Yes, yes, and I thought you were dead, as I could get no reply. You are as difficult to come at as a grand sultan.

Cod. I am a grand sultan. I rejoice in a plurality of wives. Oh, that Turkey, what a blessed country! where bigamy is a virtue, and a man's consequence is rated not by the number of voices he can command in parliament, but by the number of wives he can command at home. But tell me, how did you discover my retreat?

Lynx. You certainly could not expect to remain here unknown.

Cod. Why?

Lynx. The house not only belongs to an inspector of the police, but a Bow-street officer occupies the floor above you.

Cod. Oh! I am a doomed man. (*falling into his chair*)

Lynx. The woman of the house gave me your whole history, when I called a quarter of an hour ago. I expect two or three of our friends here in a moment. Dismal, I have left at the door.

Cod. Which do you think the easiest method of quitting life?

Lynx. Quitting life!

Cod. Aye, of committing suicide?—hanging, poisoning, suffocation, drowning, or the pistol? For to one of these escapes from my terrors, I am determined to apply.

Lynx. Then you have not seen your wife?

Cod. Which?

Lynx. Your second.

Cod. Not since we parted at your house yesterday. I can never face her again. How is Mrs. Lynx?

Lynx. She has left me.

Cod. Left you?

Lynx. I am now in search of her, for this morning I have received intelligence that leaves me at liberty to confess more respecting the girl than I have hitherto dared to tell.

Cod. That girl! My adopted daughter, you mean?

Lynx. I do; to this alone is my wife indebted for my seeking her. I would rather have died, than have been the first to advance one step towards a reconciliation, after her deliberate attempt yesterday at publicly exposing me.

(a knock heard again at L. D.*)*

Cod. There's somebody else, who can it be?

Lynx. 'Tis no doubt, Dismal, our brother in misfortune.

Cod. Misfortune!

Lynx. He and his wife have also separated. Indeed, I hear that of the whole party of married people that sat down to my table yesterday, not one couple are now living together.

Cod. They found my example so very pleasant, I suppose that they could not resist following it. *(knocking again.)*

Young. *(without)* Open the door, we wish to see you.

(LYNX *unbolts the door*—YOUNGHUSBAND *and* DISMAL **enter.**)

Young. *(to* CODDLE*)* Ah, my friend, we have found you out at last.

Dis. Mr. Dove is below, and wants to see you.

Cod. He sha'n't come in; I won't have any more visitors. I came here to conceal myself, and here is my whole circle of acquaintances around me already; well, sit down, sit down, as you *are* here. *(they all sit)* What poor unhappy wretches we all are!

Young. For my own part, I freely confess that I never was more miserable in all my days, and really begin to think that a wife is an indispensable comfort.

Cod. Where you've but one. 'Tis a comfort so peculiarly singular, that once pluralized, it is destroyed.

Dis. I had no idea that a restless night, by myself, could have made me think so favorably of Mrs. Dismal.

Lynx. Ah, my friends, absence, like death, leads us to dwell on the better qualities of those that are away.

Cod. And the heart that can then but refer to faults, is one of which we ought to be ashamed. If the second Mrs. Coddle had but consulted my comforts a little more than she did, and not look'd for raptures and passions in one who had them not in his nature—she would have been a divinity.

Young. *My* wife's great fault is her perpetual proneness for contradiction; were she to qualify her opposition, by presuming that I mistake, or by merely thinking that I am wrong, I should be satisfied; but her flat contradictions on every subject are unbearable, and I won't put up with it; she sometimes makes me quite furious, zounds!

Dis. *My* wife's great defect is her want of cheerfulness; and expecting me every moment to be petting her like a Dutch pug. I can't fondle and be continually my dearing; my amiable moments are periodical.

Cod. We are all wretched creatures and I'm the most wretched among you ; *you may* be reconciled some day or other, but for me—I am without hope. (*knocking at the door*, L. D.) Hush !— who's there ? (*going to the door.*)

Dove. (*without*) It's me.

Cod. Who ?

Dove. Mr. H. Dove.

Cod. You can't come in.

Dove. I want to speak to Mr. Coddle, on a *pint* of vast *prominence* to him.

Dis. I forgot to tell you he was asking for you when I came up ; he says that he has something to relate respecting your first wife.

Cod. What can it be ? Shall I let him in ?

Lynx. Yes, yes.

CODDLE *opens the door ;* DOVE **enters** ; CODDLE *closes the door again, and bolts it.*

Dove. Ha ! how d'ye do, gentlemen all ? We meet again, under very *conspicious* circumstances.

Cod. Sit down, sir. (*placing a chair, and going to his seat.*)

Dove. We're all bachelors again, I hear ; I ain't seen Mrs. Dove since yesterday ; she worked upon my feelings, and *aspirated* me to that degree, that I went and got *cummy fo ;* and now I am afraid to go home.

Cod. Well, sir ! this information—

Dove. Yes, sir,—but first allow me to collect my loose memorandums. My head's a little *circumfused.*

Lynx. Proceed, sir, I beg ; consider Mr. Coddle's anxiety.

Dove. Well then—you must know—yesterday—after you had all gone, Mrs. D. exaggerated me to such a pitch, that I flew out of the house—never intending to be united again.

Cod. Well !

Dove. As I was rushing through the streets—resolved to do as I liked—and talk as I liked, and to remove every *obelisk* that stood in my way of so doing, who should I run against but a lady in black——

Cod. (*starting up*) Ah !

Lynx. Sit still, and hear him out.

Dove. Bless me, says *I*, why, ma'am, I know you ; pray ain't we united by ties of *iniquity ?* She looked at me—I looked at her, and she became *mutilated* to the spot——

Cod. Go on, go on.

Dove. Aunt, says I—

Cod. Aunt !

Dove. Aunt, says I—ain't you afraid of being *exercised*, and taken before the *conjugal* authorities ?

Cod. For what ? tell me for what ?

All. Hush, hush ! Silence.

Lynx. Proceed, Mr. Dove.

Dove. Henry, says she, I am here on a matter that demands me to be very *circumflex*, and I beg you will not make known to any one that you have met me. Aunt, says I—I owe you a grudge ; do you remember how you used to use me, when I cleaned the boots in that family where you was cook ?——

Cod. Lord ! cook ? Go on.

Dove. But to *alleviate* a long story, suffice it to say—that I found out she calls herself——

Cod. Mrs. Samuel Coddle !

Dove. Yes ; she went out to the West Indies, in a doctor's family, on account of some unlawful *willanies*. She went to Antigua——

Cod. True.

Dove. And changed her name——

Cod. Changed her name ! To what—to what ?

Dove. To—I forget—Bel——

Cod. Belvidera Montemar ?

Dove. That's it.

Cod. Then her real name was——

Dove. Jane Hobbs.

Cod. Huzza, huzza !—an illegal marriage ! I'm free—it can be put aside ! It can be put aside ! Tol de rol lol. (*dancing*) You hear, she was obliged to leave the country ; she imposed upon me ; she's left me ; she's here but to annoy me—but I'm free. Lynx unbolt the door, and let me out. (LYNX *unbolts the door*) Mr. Dove, let me collar you ; you shall never leave me till I have seen and satisfied the lawful Mrs. Coddle. You are my witness, and must come to your aunt and then to my wife ; follow us, my dear friends—follow us ; seek your wives and be reconciled ; I'll set you the example. Don't attempt to get away from me ; (*to* DOVE) you are my best friend, and I shall never quit my hold of you. I wouldn't part with you for a million of money. My dear friend, my preserver, my everything on earth to me—come with me to your aunt, to Belvidera—never mind hat, coat, anything. My dear, my only Mrs. Coddle, open your arms, and receive your husband, and his friend. (*rushing out*, L. D., *and dragging* DOVE *with him by the collar.*)

Lynx. (*calling after him*) Coddle, my dear fellow, where are you running ?—let us follow him, my friends and assist each other in search of our wives, and do our best to obtain mutual forgiveness. (**Exit**, LYNX, L. D.)

Dis. I won't—I've been used very ill—I walked before my house for an hour this morning, and though Mrs. D. was seated at the window, she wouldn't turn her head to notice me.

Young. Where *my* wife can be I am at a loss to guess. Not at her aunt's ; I have been there, and they have not seen her.   I am getting quite distracted.

Dis. So am I.

Young. Then give me your arm ; if you won't go home to *your* wife you must and shall help me to regain mine.   It is a man's duty, sir, to advance the first step toward a reconcilia-tion.

Dis. I have advanced.

Young. You have not.

Dis. Didn't I walk in to the house ?

Young. No.

Dis. I did, and I won't go again.

Young. You shall.   If you don't know your duty, I'll teach it you.   Come, sir, come.

(**Exit** YOUNGHUSBAND *dragging off* DISMAL, L. D.)

Scene II.—*A Room at a Boarding House.*

Enter MRS. LYNX, *followed by* MRS. CODDLE, MRS. YOUNG-HUSBAND, MRS. DISMAL, *and* MRS. DOVE, R. 1 E.

Mrs. Cod. (*to* MRS. DISMAL) The unhappy creature, Mrs. Belvidera Coddle, is lodging here, you tell me ?

Mrs. Dis. Yes, 'twas at the door of this house that I saw Mr. Lynx talking to her yesterday.

Mrs. Cod. As she is not within, I shall look in again. I am re-solved to see her, for the more I reflect, the more I am incensed against my husband.   Oh ! I am wretched woman.

Mrs. Ly. Indeed, I am.

Mrs. Dove. So am I.

Mrs. Dis. So am I.

Mrs. Y. I'm completely miserable—miserable.

Mrs. Cod. I went home, but Coddle never came near the house ; he has absconded, no doubt ; I did not close my eyes all night.

Mrs. Dove. I have been in a state of perfect distraction since my unhappy disagreement with Henry—where *can* he have gone ?

Mrs. Y. I would not go to my aunt—I changed my mind, called on Mrs. Dismal, and sat up with her, I am determined not to return home till Frederick fetches me ; it *was* Uncle Tol-loday that gave me that thimble.

Mrs. Dis. If you had not come to me, Mrs. Y., I should have died before morning ; as it is, Mr. D.'s cruel indifference has worn me to a shade.

Mrs. Cod. Indifference ! I'm sure the apathy of my husband was never equalled ; I have flirted with a dozen young men in one evening to excite him to a little harmless jealousy, but in vain, and I really think, he would neither have stirred, nor cared, had I eloped with three captains at once. And now to discover that he has another wife! Oh! if I could see him again—I think I should assassinate him! a monster! a—eh! (*sobbing*)

Mrs. Dis. Just like my Dismal; when we go into company, he always gets as far away from me as he can; never notices me—never smiles at me—never looks as if he loved me. I—I—I am a very illused woman. (*sobbing*)

Mrs. Y. (*sobbing*) Don't weep, Mrs. Dismal; don't weep; I won't, if—if—I break my heart. Y. sha'n't say that I ever dropped a tear at his absence—the aggravating creature; though I *could* be comfortable with him, if he would not contradict me in everything I say—and do—and—and—oh! (*crying*)

Mrs. Dove. (*sobbing*) Oh, Henry!—once reconciled, I will never correct you again; you may select your own words from any dictionary you may think proper.

Mrs. Ly. (*sobbing*) My wretched fate is fixed; I have suffered beyond the bounds of endurance, and can suffer no more.

Mrs. Cod. My friends!—ladies!—bless me, we are all in tears! this must not be; what would our husbands say if they knew of our weakness? No, no—we must not break our hearts for such creatures; we must rally and laugh. Ha! ha! ha! laugh, ladies, laugh! and make your arrangements for the future with resolution and spirit. You, Mrs. Lynx, will, I presume, for the present lodge here. I shall now step to my friend's and return in half an hour. Mrs. Dove, you are a sensible and well-educated woman; pray accompany me, and give me your advice! we may hear of Mr. Dove while we are gone. Mrs. Y., you, of course, will stay with Mrs. Dismal for the present. Good-bye my dears, good-bye! Now, pray, don't fret; be women—be women—don't weep about a man. What are men?—mere self-elected law makers. Don't despair, ladies; the time is fast coming when *we* shall have voices in the legislation of the country, and then let them look to their questions. The wrongs done to our sex for centuries, shall be well revenged in the first session. (**Exit** *with* MRS. DOVE, L.)

Mrs. Y. Good-bye, Mrs. Lynx; if you wish to see us, we are only next door to you, you know. And pray, if you hear anything of our husbands, apprize us immediately, and we will do the same for you. (*taking* MRS. DISMAL'S *arm*) Now, if Mr. Dismal passes the house again, I *will* call him in.

Mrs. Dis. No, no; you shall not.

Mrs. Y. I *will*.

Mrs. Dis. I won't hear of it.

Mrs. Y. I'm not used to contradict, but you must. Though I am wretched, if I can assist in restoring happiness to others, Mrs. Frederick Younghusband is not the woman to be idle in such a matter. So come, dear D., smile and look pleasant! (**Exit**, *with* MRS. DISMAL, L.)

Mrs. Ly. (*alone*) Now, what course shall I take?—that my husband is guilty, I have abundant proof—and that I can never, never live with him again, is equally sure. I have sought a refuge here, in a miserable lodging-house; for where had I to go? Where *could* an outraged and homeless wife seek for shelter? with friends—with relations? No, no; I could not endure that bitter humiliation. If I am to be wretched, it shall be unseen and alone; I'll have no cold and affected sympathy—no pity from my kindred. Pity! there is no such feeling! 'tis disguised triumph, and we know it too; else why does the soul rise up within us and spurn it? (*looking off* R. I E.) Ah, *he* here! the writer of the letter I received yesterday? then he has traced me to this house. What shall I do? he must not see me. Hark! (*listens*) he is making inquiries concerning me; how shall I avoid him? To retaliate upon my husband, I affected to encourage that man, and he thus presumes upon it. But now, though I shall never return again to my home, I must avoid all that would make me cease to respect myself—I'll to my room.

(**Exit**, R. I E.)

Enter LYNX, L.

Lynx. I have been rightly informed, my wife *is* here. Now that I have no further occasion for secrecy, she shall know all; and if I *can* awaken her to a sense of the mischiefs that will arise from a too watchful jealousy, I will henceforth pursue that line of conduct which must and shall ensure happiness. (*he is going*, R.) What! who is that? (*looking off*) He speaks to my wife— she repulses him—he follows her, the villain! (LYNX *rushes off* R. CODDLE *is heard without*, L.)

Cod. Come along, Dove, come along; my wife is here. Come my best friend—my preserver.

Enter CODDLE, *dragging* DOVE; DOVE'S *coat is torn, and he strives in vain to release himself from the grasp of* CODDLE.

Cod. Huzza! huzza! you've told the truth, Dove—you've told the truth—Belvidera has retreated and left me master of the field. Be grateful, you villain, be grateful. She would have torn your eyes out, murdered you, had it not been for me.

Dove. But, Mr. Coddle, my coat is separating; let me go.

Cod. No, no, I must now introduce you to my wife. Where is she? Mrs. Coddle! (*calling*) Mrs. Coddle! They told me she was here ; where are you, my dear, where are you ? She can't be in the house ; then we'll run all over London but we'll find her. Come, Dove, my friend, my preserver come.

Dove. Oh, Mr. Coddle, let me go, let me go.

Cod. No, no, I'll never part with my witness ; come, you delightful fellow, come, you shall never leave me till I am restored to happiness. (CODDLE *during the foregoing exclamations, has dragged* DOVE *round the stage and goes off with him again,* L.)

Scene III.—*A gallery in the Boarding House.* LYNX *heard within.*

Lynx. (*within*) Villain ! Villain ! what do you here ? (*a noise as of a struggle ; a scream heard*) I am unarmed, or you should not leave this alive ; come, Emmeline, come with me.

Enter LYNX, *dragging out his wife ; she is pale and agitated.*

Mrs. Ly. Ah, Lionel—is it you, is it you ? Oh, bless you, bless you. (*taking his hands—he places her in a chair*) I have brought this upon myself.

Lynx. But you are safe ; and who has saved you ?

Mrs. Ly. (*falling on his neck*) My husband !

Lynx. Stay you here, I *will* follow him and have revenge.

Mrs. Ly. (*clinging to him*) Nay, nay, I implore you, stay near me—about me—leave me not again.

Lynx. But I have now a clue to him, which I will not forsake till his heart's blood atones for my injuries.

Mrs. Ly. Do you know him, that you speak thus ?

Lynx. I do, indeed.

Mrs. Ly. Who—and what is he ?

Lynx. Who ? listen, Emmeline ; the deceiver of my sister, and the father of that girl, through whom we separated and thus meet again.

Mrs. Ly. The father !

Lynx. I dared not confess as much before. I was bound, sworn to secrecy by my sister ; but her death now makes me free to tell you all.

Mrs Ly. Forgive me—I—I am satisfied.

Lynx. You shall first know that you have good cause to be so ; that villain in early life wronged my sister ; she afterwards married ; had her previous intimacy with this man been known, ruin, in the noble sphere in which she moved, must have awaited her ; I kept her secret religiously, and, as you know, at the expense of my own peace ; I was as a father to the girl ; and though she left the asylum in which I placed her, yet 'twas for an honorable and a happy marriage.

Mrs. Ly. No more, no more, dear Lionel : I have been a weak and foolish woman, but never will I doubt you again.

Lynx. And never more, dear Emmeline, will I give you cause ; on the conduct of the husband chiefly rests the virtue of the wife, and I here renounce all my follies for ever. But for that villain——

Mrs. Ly. Nay, nay, be satisfied, be at peace ; and let mutual confidence henceforth secure to us that happiness to which we have so long been strangers.

Lynx. It shall, Emmeline, it shall. (*they embrace*)

Enter MR. *and* MRS. YOUNGHUSBAND *and* MR. *and* MRS. DISMAL, *arm in arm, and laughing,* MRS. DOVE *following.*

Mrs. Y. What ! Mr. and Mrs. Lynx, and embracing too : then you have explained and made it up, as we have done. Well, this is delightful ! Mr. and Mrs. Dismal are friends ; I saw him watching his house ; I rushed out—dragged him in.— Y., who was with him, followed ; we pouted a little—coquetted a little—cried a little—and then rushed into each other's arms ; didn't we, Frederick ?

Young. No, I——

Mrs. Y. Hush ! remember, dear ; you have promised never to contradict me again.

Mrs D. And my George has vowed to be as kind, and as attentive in future, as——

Dis. As I can.

Mrs. Y. There is poor Mrs. Dove in an agony about her Henry. She left Mrs. Coddle—came to us—was told that her husband was in this house—and he is still nowhere to be found.

Lynx. We heard both he and Mr. Coddle were here not long since.

Dove. (*without*) Martha !

Mrs. Dove. Ah ! I hear his welcome voice.

Enter DOVE, *his clothes torn to ribbons.*

Dove. Martha ! are you here ? Oh, look at me.

Mrs. Dove. Henry ! look at me, and forgive me.

Dove. Forgive you, Martha ! yes, that I will, after what I've suffered since our abduction. This is all Mr. Coddle's doings ; I was his witness, and he wouldn't let me leave him till I had seen aunt Hobbs and Mrs. Coddle, in his presence. We have seen 'em ; aunt Hobbs is gone off again ; and Mr. and Mrs. Coddle are coming here with all their differences *re-united.*

Mrs. Dove. Your aunt Hobbs !

Dove. Don't ask questions now, dear ; when we are alone I'll liquidate everything.

Mrs. Dove. Elucidate !

Dove. Now, you are going to begin again, love !

Mrs. Dove. No, Henry, I forgot myself ; I never shall correct you, more, dear.

Enter CODDLE, *capering, dressed in a suit of nankeen ;* MRS. CODDLE, *on his arm.*

Cod. Here we are ! here we are ! Belvidera has retreated in confusion ; and the conquering hero, with his only lawful wife, stands before you in all the conscious pride of innocence, and a complete suit of Nankeen.

All. Nankeen !

Cod. Yes ; no lining—no, Mrs. Coddle has heard all—and has forgiven all ; she is now convinced how I was duped by my first wife ; has had proof of her leaving me—of her plundering me—of her coming here merely to make a property of me—of the illegality of the marriage ; and here we are united and happy again ; and there stands my friend and preserver, of whom I shall ever think with gratitude. (*pointing to* DOVE)

Dove. Then allow me to observe, while you were pillaging your wardrobe, your gratitude might have jogged your memory a little, respecting the condition of your preserver's clothes ; this is quite the result of your own exuberance.

Mrs. Dove. My dear Henry——

Cod. Hush, Mrs. Dove ; allow your husband to select his own words at pleasure—yield a little to each other, 'tis the best and only way to secure domestic peace. I shall yield everything. Look at me ; I that three days ago was all flannel and under-waistcoats, now intend to defy air, draughts, open-windows, corner-houses, everything ; and I and Mrs. Coddle are going in search of the North Pole. Lynx, my boy, have you cleared up your mystery and satisfied your wife ?—that's right, now let us forgive and forget ; forget all but those qualities that first in-duced us to marry. Mrs. Sam, what did you have me for ?

Mrs. Cod. Because I could discover, through all your eccen-tricities, a natural goodness of heart.

Cod. Then whenever you are inclined to be angry with me, always think of that, and I, in return, will ever remember the af-fection that first led me to seek you. Lynx, what did you marry for ?

Lynx. I freely confess it was for love.

Cod. And you, Mrs. Lynx, married him from the same im-pulse ?

Mrs. Ly. Yes, sir.

Cod. And you, Mr. and Mrs. Younghusband, married——

Young. For the same reason, as our friends Mr. and Mrs. Lynx married.

Mrs. Y. For the same reason precisely.

Cod. And you, Mr. Dismal ?

Dis. Because I was tired of living alone.

Cod. And Mrs. D. was weary of the same life, no doubt ?

Mrs. Dis. I confess my weakness.

Cod. And you, Mr. and Mrs. Dove, married—because—

Mrs. Dove. Being a widow, and accustomed to a sharer in my joys and sorrows——

Dove. You took me into partnership, at my master's dissolution.

Cod. Well, then, whenever a disagreement breaks out among you in future, recall the memory of those inducements which first led you to think of each other, and you will find it to be a wonderful help to the restoration of peace. Do you all agree to this !

All. Yes, yes.

Cod. Then follow my example, and ratify the agreement by a hearty conjugal embrace ; *I* will give the word of command Make ready !

As CODDLE *puts his arm round his wife's waist, each of the husbands does the same to his wife.*

Present !

CODDLE *takes his wife's chin between his fingers and thumb, and prepares to kiss her—all the husbands do the same.*

Fire !

(they all kiss and embrace at the same moment.)

Cod. There, this is the way that all matrimonial quarrels should end ; and if *you* are of the same opinion, *(to the audience)* then, indeed will our conjugal joy be complete, and our light lesson not have been read in vain.   You have seen the result of perpetual jealousy, in the case of Mr. and Mrs. Lynx ; of continual disputes and contradiction in that of Mr. and Mrs. Younghusband ; of a want of cheerfulness in Mr. and Mrs. Dismal ; of the impolicy of public correction, in the instance of Mrs. Dove ; and of the necessity of assimilating habits and tempers in the singular case of Mr. and Mrs. Coddle.   And though these may not be one half the cause of quarrel between man and wife—yet, even their exposure may serve as beacon lights, to avoid the rocks of altercation, when sailing on the sea of matrimony.   So think of us, all ye anticipating and smiling single people ; for you *must* or *ought*, all to be married, and the sooner the better

—and remember us, ye already paired ; and let our example prove to you, that, to mutual forbearance, mutual confidence mutual habits, mutual everything, must we owe mutual happiness.   And where can the *best* of happiness be found, but in a loyal and affectionate MARRIED LIFE.

DISPOSITION OF THE CHARACTERS.

Mr. L. Mrs. L. Mr. Y. Mrs. Y. Mr. C. Mrs. C. Mr. D. Mrs. D. Mr. Do. Mrs. Do.

CURTAIN.